FIREWORKS
Over
TOCCOA

ALSO BY JEFFREY STEPAKOFF

Billion-Dollar Kiss

FIREWORKS

Over

TOCCOA

Jeffrey Stepakoff

**Doubleday Large Print
Home Library Edition**

THOMAS DUNNE BOOKS

St. Martin's Press

New York

THOMAS DUNNE BOOKS.
An imprint of St. Martin's Press.

Music Corp. and the Johnny Mercer Foundation.
All rights on behalf of the Johnny Mercer Foundation
administered by WB Music Corp. All rights reserved.
Used by permission of Alfred Publishing Co., Inc.

ISBN 978-1-61664-267-9

FOR ELIZABETH

Author's Note

In the fall of 2003, I made a trip to Lawrence County, Pennsylvania, to research a TV pilot about a multigenerational fireworks family. Known as the Fireworks Capital of America, Lawrence County is still home to some of the world's biggest pyrotechnics companies. These are family-owned businesses that brought their art and craft with them from Italy a century ago.

Most memorably, I had dinner in a local restaurant with George Zambelli, founder of the great Zambelli Fireworks Internationale, his wife, Connie, and his daughters.

What I didn't know at the time was that George was dying. When I read about his passing a few weeks later, I understood why he had been so candid and emotional during my interview with him at dinner. And why Connie cried through much of it.

He talked a great deal about the magic of his work and the "engraving effect" of fireworks. As I listened to him speak with great passion and zest (even as sick as he evidently was) and watched the way he looked at his wife of sixty years, it was clear to me that Connie was the inspiration for George's magic. This was the only woman George Zambelli ever loved, and his work, I believe, whether for presidents, popes, or Pittsburghers, was a constant tribute to her.

The pilot did not go into production, but I had stumbled onto a story that I couldn't let go of. And the more I continued following it, the more I realized that it was in fact much deeper than I originally suspected.

What follows is inspired by my original research in Lawrence County, especially in the town of New Castle, as well as extensive interviews conducted a few years later in and around Toccoa, Georgia. What could not be learned, what voids remained in the narrative, I filled with what I know to be true from my own heart.

—Jeffrey Stepakoff
Fall 2009

There are no ordinary lives.
—Ken Burns

**A moment in the sky, forever
in the heart.**
—Ernesto Russo

DISCOVERY

Toccoa, Georgia, 2007

The two boys rode their mountain bikes along the soft uncovered lake bed between the Bartam's Field subdivision and the old Holly Hills property.

In 1955, the Army Corps of Engineers dammed the Savannah River, creating Lake Hartwell and flooding nearly fifty-six thousand acres, pretty much everything for miles along the Georgia–South Carolina border. There were stories of people refusing to give up their land—some reportedly met work crews with shotguns—but in the end, the government won out. The low-lying pine forests were cut down and any outbuildings in the floodplains hastily bulldozed. Where creeks once rambled through quiet woods to the northeast of Toccoa, gated golfing communities now rimmed the wide fingers of the massive artificial reservoir.

This history was lost on the two boys. To them the lake was simply a backyard, a place for waterskiing and motorboating, a selling point for the area's multitudinous new developments spiraling out from the waterfront. But the record drought that had plagued Georgia since mid-2006 now made water sports, and even swimming in some areas, potentially hazardous. Rotting sorrel stumps jutted through the water. Mud-covered rocks lay exposed.

So on this day, because playing in the water was not an option, the two ten-year-olds rode their bikes along the dirt of the lake bed that had been submerged just a few months ago. It was sludgy and uneven, and though their knobby tires were designed for such things, riding was difficult. The muddy moonscape was peppered with granite and decayed roots and the occasional beer can oxidized through with rust.

As they were navigating and trying to maintain enough speed to stay upright, something caught their eyes. A glint of metal. A shiny sparkle off glass.

They fishtailed their bikes to a stop. Both looking intently, they saw sunlight reflecting off something wedged under a stack of large, smooth river stones. The low waterline lapped at the stones, the sort the boys had seen imbedded in chimneys in multimillion-dollar faux-rustic cabins.

They dismounted their bikes, dropped them, and headed toward the river-stone pile, following the glistening light that shone off something that looked very much out of place here. It was something that no one had seen for more than six decades—something that, if not for this record drought, may never have been seen again, as the cabin and its bulldozed river-stone chimney had been underwater since the summer of 1955.

A PERFECT HOUSE

**Buckhead district of Atlanta,
six months later**

And I think we should get pregnant right away," Drew Candler said, turning off Peachtree onto a tree-lined side street.

"We?" Colleen turned in the leather bucket passenger seat and playfully raised an eyebrow at him.

"Well, I'm a participant in this process, too."

"So you'll be carrying a bowling ball in *your* belly?"

"I'll be rubbing your back."

"Will you be changing diapers?"

"Every chance I get."

"Midnight feedings?"

"Wouldn't miss 'em."

"And what happens when you're on call?"

"Nannies."

She couldn't help but laugh. He always had the right answer to everything. "See, this is why my friends' husbands hate you."

"Because I'm the sensitive type."

"You're raising the bar too high for these poor guys."

He feigned a worried expression. "Oh man, you didn't tell anyone about the little love notes, did you?"

"Well . . ."

"I'm gonna get whacked," he joked. "They're gonna invite me out for a beer and beat me. I can see this coming."

Drew drove up to the front gates of an elegant new housing development, punched a code into the call box, and drove in as the gates opened.

"Hey, I've told them about your affinity for lying around all Sunday in your boxers watching football and eating nachos, but I get no sympathy."

"I can be more of a jerk. Really, I know I can."

"I know, my dear. You can do anything

you set your mind to. That's one of the things I love about you. But I'm good with the football and the nachos."

He broke into a broad smile and turned his eyes toward Colleen for a moment, taking her in as he had from the first day he saw her. She was so beautiful, he thought, as he always did. Even with her black hair pulled back in a casual ponytail away from her dark eyes as she had it today. How could anyone look at her and not think the same thing? Somehow this notion was reassuring to him.

They pulled up in front of an expansive new house, a little too big for its lot but stunning nonetheless. Where once a single ranch-style home sat on two wooded acres, there were now nine estate homes. Hundreds of containers of azaleas and dogwoods and Cherokee roses, ubiquitous in these kinds of North Atlanta communities, were lined up along the curb, ready to be planted in the smallish yards.

"What do you think?"

"Wow." She just stared at the residence, at a loss to articulate any kind of detailed response.

"'Wow' is right. Come on."

Drew hopped out, jogged over to Colleen's side of the newly leased luxury sedan, and opened the door for her. With a boyish glee that belied his tall build, he grabbed her arm and marched her up the front walkway and through the open front door. They were hit with the intoxicating scent of fresh paint, new appliances, and sawdust.

He watched as she took in the house.

"Five bedrooms up. One below. And the master suite is off the main, around that way," he said, pointing. "Oh, and just off the kitchen, over there, they call it a family studio."

Colleen peered into a large room with washer-dryer hookups, a worktable, a message center desk with cell-phone docks, and three built-in child-size lockers with coat hangers and space for boots and books.

"There's room for more than three lockers. You know, just in case one ever wanted to expand." Drew couldn't be happier.

Colleen continued looking around at the house for a long time. It was as though Drew had extrapolated everything she had ever mentioned in passing about the future and what he had seen on the dog-eared pages of the house and style magazines she'd recently been perusing and what he heard discussed at dinner parties and golf outings and silent auction cocktail events by those who had their names on wings of buildings vital to the community, and then put it all together and come up with this house. Her friends would most likely describe the house in the same terms they talked about Drew. It was an ideal house.

However, to stand awake in the middle of such a thing, to hear the wraithlike echoes of children to be born and days to be lived and nights to be pondered among these planked halls, was to stand in the future, to see it and know it plainly. No more hazy morning daydreams about what life might be. No more giddy talk over lattes or margaritas. This was it.

It was a gorgeously plated meal that was ordered for her, one she was reluctant to disturb with immutable matters rendered by the fork, but even more loath to send back untouched. What Drew happily took for overwhelming excitement was in fact apprehension over the sudden reality set before her.

She hadn't known him for very long, but what she did know seemed very right. Whatever doubts or questions she might have had about the future and what she wanted out of it were always allayed by his certainty. He was always so sure about everything, about a life that would be very much like that of the most senior partners in his practice, and about how she fit seamlessly into that. Along with his other attributes, Drew possessed a kind of confidence that could sweep a girl off her feet. But there was something about standing here in this house that made her realize how quickly the future was happening, and just how little thought, of her own, she'd really given it.

His BlackBerry rang and involuntarily he snapped it off his belt and answered it. "Yes. . . . How many centimeters? . . . Yes, that's fine, page the anesthesiologist. I'll be there in thirty minutes." He hung up and snapped the phone back on its belt cradle.

"I have to get to Northside. I'll drop you on the way."

"You go ahead. I'll call the office and

have someone pick me up. I want to stay here for a little while."

"You know, it might be time to give them your notice."

"We'll talk about that."

"Whatever you want. I just hate seeing you working at a job you don't need or love."

He gave her a kiss.

"When I saw this place and thought about us here," he said, "I felt like all the pieces were just snapping into place. So what do you think?"

"What do I think?"

"About the house! Do you like it?"

"It's amazing."

"But?"

"No but."

"Come on, Colleen. This is your fiancé you're talking to. What's wrong with the house?"

"Honestly . . . ," she said, looking around, searching for words to describe her complicated feelings. She settled on simple truth. "Absolutely nothing. It's perfect. It's a perfect house."

"Good. Because I put an offer in last night." He gave her a broad smile and then walked out, his footsteps echoing as she stood alone in the enormous empty house.

Watching him hurry down the walkway and hop in his new car, Colleen wondered what was wrong with her. She never had a problem committing to things. She made plans weeks in advance, bought multiyear magazine subscriptions, she was someone who turned in term papers *early*. She knew how to make choices and act on them. Then again, this house, she wasn't really being asked to make much of a choice about it.

But how much did that matter?

Lifting her head, she rotated it again. Yes, it was like looking at a model home picked out for a magazine shoot. So what was the problem? What else was there beyond perfect? What was there to think about?

LILY

Toccoa, a few days later

What could you say to a young woman who thought she was in love when you thought she might be making the biggest mistake of her life? Lily chewed on this as she waited for her granddaughter.

Lily sat in a comfortable chair on her wraparound porch, looked out at the Blue Ridge foothills, and drank her morning Coke. It was in the traditional curved glass bottle, upon which the tiny words HECHO EN MEXICO were affixed. Every month since July of 1988, when the Georgia bottlers started using corn syrup, Lily had driven to a small Hispanic-owned shop in Gainesville and bought her stash of Mexican-bottled Coca-Cola, which was still made with cane sugar.

Lily liked living alone. She missed her husband, of course. But since his passing four years ago, an odd kind of restfulness had made its way into her days. She often told herself that this was simply the opportunity provided by more time on her hands. But deep down, she knew it was something more. It was as though the seams of her life had been let out just a bit.

Eighty-two years old, living alone in her big house, Lily was lonely at times. But this was a feeling, an exquisite bittersweetness, that she didn't entirely mind. Simply put, Lily was at peace.

Her residence, a white Queen Anne–style classical revival, was built in 1901 on a hill just north of town. It was initially used as a "summerhouse" for well-to-do boarders escaping the heat in Atlanta. In July, during the day, they would sit out on this sprawling porch in high-backed white rocking chairs, sipping sweet peach tea and enjoying the cool Appalachian breezes. And at night they would drink gin and tonic and marvel at the wonder of a billion stars over Toccoa. Since then, everything had changed, and not much had changed. The world was such a different place, but there were the same stars, the same kinds of yearnings beneath them.

Lily watched as a large car pulled up the hill and parked in front of her house. Stretching her legs after the hour-and-a-half drive up from the city, Colleen got out of the shiny new sedan, which Lily thought was way too big and stuffy for her granddaughter. But these kinds of vehicles were apparently one of the enviable perks of working in sales for a huge pharmaceutical company.

"Grandma, the kudzu is nearly up to your front porch!" Colleen said as she bounded up the walkway in front of the house.

"It's fine. I just trimmed it back this week." The broad-leafed vine made its way out of the woods behind the house but was cut before it could invade the lawn.

"Why don't you just have the gardeners get rid of it once and for all?" Colleen scooped up the newspaper resting on one of the stone steps leading to the porch. "You'll wake up one morning and you won't be able to get out your front door."

"You leave my kudzu alone. We have an understanding." Lily grabbed her granddaughter, hugged her quickly, and then held her back for examination.

"How's life in the fast lane?" said Lily.

"Fast. In fact, I can't stay too late. One of Drew's partners bought a table at this silent auction black-tie thing at the Grand Hyatt tonight."

Lily noticed that Colleen made very little effort to hide her lack of enthusiasm for the event. A million things rushed through Lily's mind, but she just smiled.

"You ready to see it?" Lily said.

Colleen took a deep breath and nodded.

Lily had been cooking earlier in the day and the inside of the house smelled of something wonderful, risotto with summer vegetables, Colleen guessed. Lily was a famously good cook and Colleen always came here hungry, knowing she would be fed something simple but sublime.

Colleen loved the inside of this house as much as she loved the porches outside. In fact, with its massive quarter-sawn paneling, heavy oak pocket doors, lacquered walnut flooring, fine dentil molding, grandly carved staircase, and various fireplaces with their immense hardwood mantels, there was something about being surrounded by all this natural wood that made one feel right in the middle of nature, connected to it, even though it was all inside. They simply didn't make houses like this anymore, and being here always transported Colleen from where she was in her life to a place where she could reflect on it. Along with the house, its connectedness to nature and history, her grandmother's steadiness, and the small-town ease of Toccoa all contributed to make this a place of peace and perspective for Colleen.

Lily set the long rectangular box down on a knit rug in the center of the living room floor. Box cutter in hand, she slowly knelt beside it. Colleen just sat quietly, letting her grandmother tend to this long-awaited task. Colleen looked around the room, filled with memories of all the times over the years she had heard reference to the contents of this box rushing over her.

Along with framed photographs of a life well lived, the living room was filled with art. Colleen had been in this room so often since she was a little girl, but she never ceased being amazed by the fascinating pieces collected by Lily over the years. These were not the cold "fine art" paintings and objects that wealthy collectors mounted in their homes as evidence of business conquests and participation in the lineage of old money. Lily's house was filled with what could best be described as folk art: vibrantly painted religious visions by Rev. Howard Finster, colorful wood-relief carvings by Eddie Owens Martin, strange and beautiful pottery by Lanier Meaders. These self-taught rural artisans whom Lily had met and befriended had been overlooked by the society matrons of high art until recently. Today some of the work was just as valuable as the Picassos that hung in Buckhead mansions, not that their financial value mattered much to Lily. Each piece was a cherished story to her, one that she was always ready to share.

Except for one piece. Perhaps the most magnificent of all. A mosaic made from broken and brightly colored pieces of glass depicting exploding blue fireworks on a starry sky. Colleen's favorite, the piece hung prominently on the wall, but Lily had very little to say about it.

With the box-cutter blade on its lowest setting, protruding barely a quarter inch from its metal casing, Lily cut the heavy cardboard container open lengthwise. With the care and certainty of a surgeon opening a rib cage, Lily inserted her weathered fingers into the incision and broke the box open.

"It's beautiful," Colleen said.

Inside the box was a wedding gown, its satin bodice lifelike and full, bursting with acid-free tissue paper. Colleen knelt on the other side of the box and ran her hand down the side of the dress. She inspected the pale silk lace. Caressed several pearl beads. Then she pulled the dress out of the box, standing to reveal its full length, the soft fabric rising from the cardboard like mist over a creek at dawn.

For a long moment, Colleen just stood there, dress in hand hanging before her, feeling quite unsettled. For as stunning as the dress was, there was something ghostly, cadaverous, about it.

Sensing this, Lily said, "You're not going to hurt my feelings if you don't like it."

"No, no, the dress is gorgeous. It's just . . . suddenly all so real. I mean, I'm really doing this."

"Yes, dear. You're really doing this," Lily said. "Unless you really don't want to."

"Of course I want to. I'm just a bit nervous about it all. That's normal."

Offered no rising inflection but a statement of fact to which retort was not welcome, Lily just looked long and hard at Colleen. There was something left unspoken between the two women—which both knew but neither needed to articulate.

"Drew is perfect, Grandma. Perfect."

Perfect. That could be the greatest flaw in the choice of a husband. Lily knew this quite well. For of course there was no such thing as perfection in marriage. Only a checklist of certain standards and attributes that, even when found in a man, are all rendered meaningless by the trials of a life together. No, joy came from somewhere that wasn't on those premarital checklists. But this was not an easy thing to explain, particularly to someone who was not asking for an explanation.

"It's your decision, dear. You can try it on. And we can get it altered for you. Or I can take it back to the dry cleaners, have it repacked, and put it back in the closet. Whatever you want to do is fine, but it's *your* decision, do you understand? About this, listen only to yourself."

Allowing her granddaughter time to absorb this, Lily picked up the pieces of the cardboard box and headed for the kitchen, where the recycling bins and cases of empty Coke bottles were kept. On her way, she also picked up the newspaper that Colleen had brought in from the porch.

In the kitchen, Lily dropped the cardboard on top of a green bin near the back door. Then she dropped the newspaper on top of the pile as well. But before she turned, something caught her eye. She picked up the still-folded *Toccoa Record* and started reading. Without taking her eye off the paper, she opened it and placed it on the table.

Resting both hands on either side of the paper, she steadied herself. Slowly, she leaned over the paper, reading even more intently. An expression somewhere between disbelief and amazement began to sweep over her face. Her mouth fell open. As she finished the article, she looked up, off, as though she were some-place else, and as this information took hold, it set into her knees, which could no longer sustain her.

"Grandma?" Colleen walked into the kitchen just as Lily stumbled back and slumped into a chair, visibly transfixed by what she had read.

Concerned, Colleen went to the table, seeing the headline of the story in front of Lily: MUSEUM DISPLAYS NEW FINDS.

"Grandma, what is it?" Colleen said.

Lily pointed to a picture in the paper. "This is mine."

LOST AND FOUND

Capt. Carol Stokes was having a good day. It wasn't even lunchtime yet and she'd had well over a dozen visitors to her little museum. Clearly, the local media efforts were paying off.

The Currahee Military Museum, as well as the office of its sponsor, the Stephens County Historical Society, was housed in an unused section of the sprawling Toccoa Train Depot. Built as the terminus for the tens of thousands of paratroopers who came to nearby Camp Toccoa for training during World War II, the depot was renovated at great expense by local area merchants a few years ago. The initial funds were not entirely difficult to garner. HBO had popularized the depot during the run of its *Band of Brothers* TV miniseries about the men of "Easy Company" who trained at Camp Toccoa. But since the show had aired several years ago and the population of World War II vets who regularly supported events and reunions at the museum continued to age, Captain Stokes thought a lot about the future. The key to both funding and public interest would be in continuing to expand the museum's holdings and continuing to publicize them.

Captain Stokes was pleased to see Colleen and Lily as they entered the museum. A young woman and her grandmother were exactly the kinds of general public patrons Stokes was hoping to see more of at her museum. As Colleen and Lily went to one of the new exhibits, Stokes watched them. Near several permanent glass cases of military trinkets and historical memorabilia, five new pieces, all recently publicized in the local press, were on display together. These included a bullet-ridden parachute used on D-day, a complete uniform worn by a member of Easy Company during the Battle of the Bulge, never-before-seen photographs taken of training jumps made on Currahee Mountain, historically significant letters written home by members of the 101st Division during their push into Germany, and a formula for an Italian weapon, an explosive shell.

Stokes quietly approached as Lily read the small plaque next to the framed formula for the explosive, believed to be a mortar or artillery-fired shell used by the "Regio Esercito," the Italian Royal Army, during World War II. It was handwritten in Italian on a six-inch-by-four-inch piece of yellowed paper. The plaque explained that the formula was discovered nearby and was believed to have been brought back from Europe, presumably by a local serviceman, around 1945. The explosive shell, the plaque explained, was called a "Stella di Lily" by the Italians, or "Lily's Star."

"Soldiers give nicknames to everything," explained Captain Stokes as she walked over to Lily and Colleen. "Especially their weapons."

"It's wrong," said Lily.

"Excuse me?"

"You've got it all wrong. This is not a weapon."

"Well, we know from the watermark that the paper comes from 1940s Italy. The writing was carefully translated by an Italian professor at Clemson, and a retired U.S. Army Ordnance Corps officer was absolutely certain that it was the formula for an explosive device." Stokes smiled politely. "The boys from the USAOC tend to know about these things. A mortar shell, in fact."

"That is correct," Lily said as she examined the writing closely. "But it was not designed for warfare. To the contrary."

People were starting to gather, listening in on the conversation. Colleen just looked at Lily with increasing unease.

"With all due respect, ma'am, we've had several highly credentialed experts agree on what this is."

"This really shouldn't be on display."

Stokes' smile became openly patronizing as she attempted to hide her discomfort with the growing audience.

"Oh, I think there is very little danger of Italian-speaking terrorists coming to Toccoa to get an old bomb formula. Now perhaps you'd like to see some of our other new displays."

Looking a little embarrassed, Colleen was starting to wonder if her grandmother had simply lost it. "Grandma, what is going on here?"

Undeterred, Lily considered Stokes, noting the officer's name tag, and continued, "Have you figured out what magnalium is doing in a weapon, Captain Stokes?"

That shut Stokes up. *Magnalium? How does this old woman know about that?* Crossing her arms as though trying to keep control of the situation, Stokes stared at Lily, assessing her. But Lily just stared right back.

Finally, Stokes continued, "Why don't you come with me, ma'am. And we can talk about this."

"I think that is a very good idea," Lily said.

"Grandma, please, what is going on?"

"Come along, dear."

Colleen shrugged, following her grandmother and Stokes toward the back of the room.

"I have to confess, the magnalium did stump the officer from Ordnance," said

Stokes, ushering Lily and Colleen into chairs at a large wooden table.

"I am sure it did," replied Lily as she took in the Historical Society office. The commodious room was cluttered with all manner of antique objects, some being readied for display, their stories to be made public; some headed for permanent storage, their accounts perhaps never known. The office looked out on the museum through big glass windows that also brought in natural light, illuminating particles of dust most likely from disparate artifacts mixing together in the rays.

"Do you think you might know something about this . . . ?"

"Lily. Please call me Lily."

"And I'm Colleen, her granddaughter."

"Yes, I know something about this," said Lily. "The formula is named for me. Lily's Star. More to the point, it belongs to me. You see, I lost it."

Stokes stared at her for quite a while, assessing and ultimately realizing that there very well could be some truth to this. "Lily, the formula was found in a container. Do you think you can tell me what kind?"

"I am sure I can. It would have been in a

glass jar, the old Hoosier style they used to make in the Midwest."

"Yes, that's right." Both Colleen and Stokes looked amazed. After a moment, Stokes rose, walked to a shelf behind her, and produced a large plastic Ziploc bag that contained an antique quart-sized ridged-glass canister jar with a tight-fitting rusted metal lid. She put it on the table in front of Lily. "Two boys found it near the lake and their families donated it to the museum."

A rush of emotion, fueled by unearthed memories, swept over Lily's face. Hands trembling perceptibly, she reached out for the canister with great care, as though it might dissolve to dust before her. Colleen had never seen her grandmother like this. Instinctively she reached out and touched Lily's arm.

Lily spoke as her eyes washed over the jar. "Stewarts was the only coffee my father drank. When coffee was being rationed during the war, he had his Stewarts shipped down on the train from Chicago in burlap sacks, ground it, and stored it in these jars. Even when nearly all the coffee in the country, as well as the aluminum for the cans, was going overseas, he had his connections. That was my father, not even a world war could keep him from getting what he wanted."

"Lily, can you tell me about the formula?"

Lily studied the old coffee canister as though it were a photo album filled with precious and irreplaceable snapshots. Finally, she looked up at Stokes. "If I can convince you that it belongs to me, will you return it?"

"I'm listening."

Beneath them, the building shook as a train roared into the station, following the exact same tracks that had transported young men from all over the country to and from this small North Georgia town, during a time when the future for so many had never been more uncertain. It was scary and tumultuous. And exciting.

HOME

June 30, 1945

Swing music blasted so loud from the kitchen radio inside that Honey Davis could hear it quite clearly as she marched up the front steps of her daughter Lily's house. Reminding herself to go easy on Lily, who was after all barely twenty years old, Honey walked across the porch and knocked loudly on the door several times. There was no response, and there most likely wasn't going to be a response, because the music was so loud that nothing else could be heard. Honey felt that familiar frustration rising inside her.

Clenching her jaw and straightening her blouse, Honey opened the door and let herself in. She nearly tripped over the unpacked boxes of newly acquired housewares still in the foyer. Lily should be much further along, thought Honey. Lily's husband would be returning in four days and the place was simply a mess.

When Paul Woodward left for the war in 1942, just a short time after marrying Lily and purchasing the house for them, Lily had moved back into her parents' home a few miles away at Holly Hills. Aside from the matter that the house was simply too big for a teenager, albeit a married one, to live in alone, maintaining a property this size for one person regardless of age was downright frivolous during wartime. However, even though she didn't live there, Lily had spent much of the last few years putting the home together. Initially, Honey tried to help, but that didn't go over so well. Lily wanted to do things her way, and she certainly put great effort into collecting wonderful items and furnishings while Paul was away. Lily acquired things that were fun, ornamental, as opposed to utilitarian. The living room was stunning. The kitchen was bare. Until very recently. There was a sudden rush to get it set up when Paul's return was announced.

Honey couldn't help but be annoyed by Lily's efforts over these years, feeling her decorating and furnishing was more hobby than household building. More girlish amusement than womanly pursuit. The fact was, although she was married and had accepted the full responsibility of adulthood, at twenty Lily was still very much a child at heart.

Honey navigated around the boxes of practical household items and made her way into the kitchen, where she found Lily bopping to the loud swing music. Hands out, locked with those of an imaginary partner, Lily danced quickly and joyfully around mounds of pots and pans.

Honey watched her for a moment. While most of the world saw a beautiful young woman who was fair, fit, and well proportioned, the graceful and poised daughter of an important Coca-Cola executive, this private Lily was precisely the Lily, unrestrained, sweating, who worried Honey so. Honey had hoped that marriage would provide the sort of structure that would channel whatever drove her daughter to dance like this into something quietly satisfied, rendering Lily, wholly and entirely, a lady of Toccoa, Georgia. But of course there hadn't been much of a marriage. Fortunately, though, like the world around them, everything was about to change.

Honey pulled the radio plug out of the wall socket. Startled by the sudden silence, Lily looked up to find her mother in her kitchen.

"You really shouldn't sneak up on me like that," said Lily, exasperation superseding embarrassment.

"And you really should be getting your home ready. Do you want your husband to come back to something that looks worse than the rubble in Berlin?"

Just rolling her eyes, Lily returned to her task of unpacking. She pulled a beautiful chrome-and-ivory-framed picture of her husband in his officer's uniform out of a box, unwrapped it, and placed it on a nearby counter. As she leaned over and started pulling china from another box, Honey picked up the picture and moved it carefully to a more prominent location in the room. Lily watched as Honey gazed at the picture for a moment, satisfied, and then bent over and took a cup and a saucer from a box, gingerly removed the packing paper, and began to put the items away. Though the act was more imposition than help, Lily tolerated it. This was a familiar dynamic, and though it was ultimately annoying to Lily, there was comfort in the familiarity.

"They go in there, Mother," said Lily, pointing to an open waist-high drawer.

"Cups and saucers in a drawer? Lily, what are you thinking? Drawers at this level are for flatware. Cups and saucers go in the upper cabinet or cupboard, hence the name, *cup*board."

"Well, in my home, Paul and I will do things our way, even if we break a few 'rules.'"

"What you'll break is all your fine coffee cups. Every time you carelessly open that drawer and they bang into each other."

"Mother—"

Honey could hear her husband's voice telling her to relax and let her daughter live her own life a bit. Staid and vigilantly professional, he was, in fact, much more like Lily than anyone really knew, except perhaps Honey.

"Suit yourself," Honey said. "Your house. Do things your way. My mouth is shut."

"Thank you."

Honey put the cup and saucer on the counter, refusing to participate in what she deemed certain madness, something she was confident her daughter would soon come to see, the hard way. Lily picked up the items and put them away in the drawer, pleased.

"Fine," said Honey, unable to stay silent. "And why not just put your pots and pans on top of the refrigerator? Or your fine linens under the sofa? Or your—"

"Mother!"

"My mouth is shut."

"Thank you."

"Lily!" Honey exclaimed, glaring at a box of salt that had spilled onto the floor. So much for keeping her mouth shut.

Honey hurried over, tore a page from a *Good Housekeeping* magazine, and swept up the salt onto the cover. She poured it in a small glass. "You can boil it off when you unpack your pots," said Honey.

"Yes, ma'am," said Lily, primarily to appease and silence her mother. After the War Between the States, when the only way to get salt was to boil the dirt from the floors of the ravaged smokehouses, pour off the water, and use the residue in the bottom of the pot, wasting salt was a sin in Georgia.

Honey opened the refrigerator, took out two Cokes, and opened them with a nearby bottle opener. Lily grabbed one, Honey the other. Unconsciously repeating one of their long-standing rituals, they both took swigs, swallowed, and took deep, calming breaths. Even with sugar rationing making Coke hard to come by throughout most of the country, Davis households always had some cold ones on hand.

Looking at Honey, Lily thought, *You'd never have known that the entire world had been at war.* It was as though time stood still for Honey Davis. She never went without nylons, and her figure showed no signs of the flour and sugar shortages that most in Toccoa endured. Most in town attributed such things to the benefits of wealth and influence, but Lily knew it was more. In her own ways, Honey worked hard for what she got. It was just that she made getting what she wanted look effortless. But Lily knew better. Lily saw that under her mother's air of entitlement was a profound resourcefulness, a will that you did not want to cross.

This was a woman whose hair, despite season or time of day or weather, was always, audaciously, perfect. Honey had been wearing a smart pageboy bob with the ends rolled under for as long as Lily could remember. During the later years of the war even Garbo and Hepburn began to eschew the bob style they had helped make fashionable, but not Honey Davis. Her tresses were always impeccably parted and curled, set and sturdy, even in the middle of summer. And Lily knew that someone who possessed what it took to maintain her hair so well in Georgia in June was not someone to be taken lightly.

Lily and Honey looked up as an oversized wasp flew into the kitchen. Honey recoiled. "Those damn yellow jackets. They are so aggressive."

Honey quickly grabbed a newspaper, rolled it up, and began swatting. This enraged the predatory wasp, which buzzed angrily around the kitchen, scaring Honey, who swatted wildly at it. The big yellow jacket landed on the counter, buzzing tentatively. Honey approached nervously, pulled back the newspaper, and just as she was about to swat at it, in a flash, Lily brought a mason jar down over the wasp, trapping it.

"Lily!"

"Now what did that yellow jacket ever do to you?"

"I don't know if you are brave or just plumb stupid. Sometimes both, I suspect."

Lily ripped off a piece of cardboard from one of the boxes, slid it under the mason jar, and carried the jar to the kitchen door. She pushed open the screen door, released the wasp, and came back inside.

Honey just watched, both amazed and annoyed. Lily was constantly doing these sorts of impulsive things that upset Honey, who was certain that Lily often behaved this way specifically for that purpose. But Honey had to confess, she admired her daughter's fearlessness, as well as her tenacity. Lily was an original.

"You know you can stay at our home tonight if you want," said Honey.

"I'll be fine, Mother."

"I know that. I'm just saying that if you need something your father and I will be in

Atlanta, so feel free to come by anytime and get what you need."

"I think you're going to miss having me under your roof," Lily teased.

Honey searched for an equally pointed retort but, finding the moment had gotten away from her, discovered herself throwing her arms around Lily and giving her a fast but unexpectedly warm hug. The embrace said more than any words either could have produced.

"I'll miss you, too, Mother. But Paul and I will be right here, right across town. And you can come see us any time you want." Lily smiled. "Well, most any time. Feel free to call first."

The women shared a laugh. Then, suddenly, a percussive *boom*, from an explosion of some sort off in the distance, gently rocked the house. "The pyrotechnics man," said Honey.

Quickly Honey and Lily went to the front door, stepped out onto the porch, and saw a massive waterfall of sparkling luminescent light, so brilliant and radiant that even in daylight it streaked much of the western sky copper and gold.

Lily watched the firework, silent and breathless.

There hadn't been a fireworks display in the area since the war started. Nearly every fireworks company in the country had switched their factory over to weapons manufacturing. Instead of making colorful pyrotechnics displays that exploded in the sky, they were making mortar shells for use on the battlefield. In 1945, many young people, particularly those from small towns, couldn't remember ever seeing a fireworks display. Lily was one of them. Though her parents assured her she had seen fireworks at Holly Hills when she was nine, her memory of it was vague. Lily wasn't sure what she actually remembered and what she simply thought she remembered from hearing about it over the years. Needless to say, Lily was very much looking forward to the display the Toccoa Ladies Auxiliary Club had arranged for the homecoming on July 4th.

The women watched as the sparks faded and fell, leaving behind gently glowing and expanding traces of quiet alabaster smoke. Honey squeezed her daughter's hand and, finally, broke the silence of the moment. "These are very fine days we have ahead of us, darling. Very, very fine days."

Lily just nodded.

"We'll be back from Atlanta in a few days. Just in time for the homecoming festivities," said Honey. "I had GiGi put the rest of your clothes in your closet, so you can pick them up any time you want."

"Yes, Mother."

"Oh, and Jenna's in town with Mark Morgan. I told her mother that you'd get in touch with her. Do that please."

"Yes, Mother." Lily made a mental note to get in touch with her old friend and then willed her mother to leave before she thought up a hundred more things for her to do.

"Oh, and Mrs. Keener is expecting you at the market. Get whatever you need and she'll put it on our bill. If you need anything else, we'll be staying at the company apartment at the Biltmore and—"

"I'll be fine, Mother. Don't worry about me."

"Of course not, dear," lied Honey as she headed down the front porch steps. "Of course not."

Lily watched her mother growing smaller as she moved down and away, under the enchanted sky.

Though the firework was gone from sight, it remained, engraved in memory. *Such a beautiful thing*, thought Lily. Why, then, did it make her feel so emotional, so . . . *melancholy*? No, it was more specific than that. It made her feel sad. Why?

Her life was perfect. She had her dream house. And her husband was finally coming home to join her in it. She'd been thinking about him so much lately.

Paul was easy to love pretty much from day one. He was so earnest and straightforward, being with him was effortless. He didn't dance, but he didn't mind if she did. In fact, whether she was dancing in the kitchen or telling an impassioned story over dinner, Paul was content just watching Lily.

Toccoa, 1941

Enjoying a lavish but casually tasteful company picnic, several well-dressed executives and their spouses ate Green Goddess salads and barbequed chicken near the back patio of the house at Holly Hills.

In the middle of the sprawling green lawn behind and away from the house at the estate, on a beautiful knit blanket, Lily, seventeen and radiant, sat next to Paul Woodward, a tall, broad-shouldered young man in a flawless blue seersucker suit and white bucks. It was a picturesque and complete sight, of which Lily was well aware.

"So tell me, Paul Woodward, what kind of a boss is my father?" said Lily with a teasing air.

"A fair one," replied Paul, holding his own with her.

"And I suppose he would be even fairer to a bright young man with a promising future who showed affection for his daughter."

"No. I wouldn't say that about Mr. Davis."

"No?" Lily clasped her hand to her chest as though shocked.

"No, but I think he'd be quite positively inclined toward a young man for whom his *daughter* showed affection."

They shared a hearty laugh. Paul leaned back on his arms, enjoying the warmth of the sun on this fine afternoon, while Lily took a sip of champagne from a fluted crystal glass with which she'd snuck off.

"Oh, I see," Lily said playfully. "So courting me until I fall simply head over heels for you is a vital part of your career ambitions?"

"Well, seeing as how we've only had two proper dates so far, getting you to agree to go to the movies with me on Saturday night was about the extent of my ambitions. My dreams, well, that's another matter."

He looked confidently into her eyes, maintaining his glance until his words took full hold of her. After a long moment, when she could feel the blood rushing to her cheeks, Lily looked away, unable to keep herself from smiling. The attraction between them was clear.

"I don't cook, you know," she said with her continued playfulness. "And my mother will tell you that I am disposed to be more than somewhat willful, particularly when it comes to having my own way about . . . well, most everything."

"I have been duly and extensively informed."

"Hmm, I'll bet you have." Lily snuck a look over her shoulder at her mother, standing next to Lily's father, off in the distance near the house. "I'll bet my mother simply adores you."

Lily was quite aware that handsome, well-mannered, well-moneyed Paul, with a very successful future ahead of him, was exactly the kind of young man her mother had always dreamed of for a son-in-law. Lily envisioned Honey visiting the Coca-Cola executive offices and interviewing young men for a special assignment. While Lily knew that her vision was part hyperbole, she was willing to bet that it was not entirely pure exaggeration.

"She's a very nice lady, your mother," said Paul.

"I suspect she's been giving you pointers about how to get me to fall for you, hasn't she?"

"She's a very nice lady, your mother," said Paul again with a smile.

"Well, in all fairness to your career ambitions and the future of my heart, Paul Woodward, you should know that I rarely agree with my mother's penchants and predilections and in fact I—"

Paul cut her off. "You have been known to make quite the effort to embrace most anything that runs contrary to her tastes and wishes."

"I see you two *have* been talking."

"Lily, I'm a simple guy," he said more seriously, showing the earnestness that was the core of his plain nature. "I did okay in college, but I probably wouldn't have gotten in without football. I understand my job, which is essentially sales, and I like it. I love the company, and I love Georgia, and that's really all I want with my life, along with someone to share it with and . . . What I mean is . . . I'm not good at talking about my inner feelings, Lily."

"You're doing just fine," she said, looking over her shoulder at her parents watching her, then turning back to Paul.

"What I mean is, taking a blow from the entire front lines of Alabama and Tech and NC State combined would be nothing compared to how hard it is not to kiss you, Lily Davis."

She took his hand and one could almost see the spark jump between them.

"So kiss me."

"Kiss you?"

"You could kiss me now, you know." She leaned in closer to him.

"Your parents are watching."

"You could still kiss me."

"That wouldn't be respectful."

"So your concerns about what others think are greater than getting smacked around by a bunch of butt-slapping linemen, and greater than your feelings for me." Lily smiled mischievously, but he was getting nervous.

"I didn't say that."

"Not to mention that kissing Walter Davis' daughter in his own backyard could have decidedly deleterious effects on a young man's career."

"Are you teasing me?"

"I am kissing you is what I am doing." She leaned in close to him, and he looked like he wasn't sure what to do. As handsome and promising and strong as the former UGA offensive tackle was, he was also no match for this younger, brighter girl who was crazy about him. "You are not the only one with inner feelings here and if you are not going to put your lips on me, which is probably very smart considering where we are, then I am going to put mine on yours, which is probably rather reckless and impetuous, but it's not going to get you fired and I simply can't bear another moment without doing so, so . . ."

And with that she kissed him. After a moment, she slowly pulled away. He looked into her eyes, and he kissed her back.

"Oh, and yes, by the way," said Lily. "Definitely yes."

"Yes to what?"

"Yes, to the movies on Saturday night," said Lily, looking as happy as can be.

Walter Davis, her father, watching from a distance, did not look as happy.

"Did I just see one of my employees kissing my daughter in my backyard?" Walter said.

"I think you just saw your daughter kissing him," replied Honey.

Honey and Walter Davis, highballs of Havana Club rum and Coke in hand, watched Lily and Paul from a distance. Walter was very tall, with a muscular build, thick, full hair graying neatly at the temples, and a jaw so impossibly long and square that at times he seemed drawn by some animator giving form to a masculine ideal. Walter had the kind of rugged good looks that could best be described as dashing, and if he'd been so inclined he would have had a very good shot at success on the silver screen, most likely as the lead in some adventure serial where he was sent around the world in a cargo plane on dangerous assignments, writing in a journal about life and death and love in understated prose and wearing a lot of khaki. Though even in such success, he most likely would not have earned as much as he did as an executive.

"I like this boy, Walter."

"Somehow I knew you would."

"You don't?"

"He's a smart kid, and a born leader, that's why I hired him."

"If there's war, I don't want him on the front lines, Walter."

"I'll find a position for him in support, maybe doing something for the company."

"What about Jonathan?"

"Jonathan has to make his own way in the world, Honey."

"I don't want my son jumping out of airplanes! Talk to him."

"I'll try again. You know I will."

Walter always knew how to speak to Honey in a way that calmed her. They sipped their drinks, watching Lily and Paul in the distance.

"I like this boy. I think he's good for her. I think he's exactly what Lily needs."

"Okay."

"You think she's too young."

"I think she's . . . Lily."

Walter put his arm around Honey, who didn't ask what he meant because she didn't really care. Her mind was made up about Paul, and Walter knew it. While he loved his little girl, Walter was a man who rarely interfered in her life. To be sure, they had wonderful easy times together when he was in town, but when it came to parenting, Honey was CEO.

A few months later

With Lily in the passenger seat of his massive 1940 Cadillac 90 town car—the company car—Paul pulled up to the front of the beautiful white 1901 Queen Anne–style house with the big wraparound porch, parked, ran around to the passenger side, and let out a surprised-looking Lily. Hair cut very short, Paul wore an Army officer's uniform.

"Why are we stopping?" asked Lily, a bit giddy.

"Come on." Paul grabbed her hand and ran her up the front walkway.

Out of breath, they stood together on the front porch, Lily looking wide-eyed at the house and the view of sky over the foothills from the front porch.

"What do you think?" said Paul.

"I think . . . I'm wondering whose house this is," said Lily, unable to contain a smile.

Paul produced a small box and handed it to her, and her smile grew until she was covering it to try to hold in the anxious laughter. Hands shaking, she took the box and then opened it. Inside was a key.

"It's my house, Lily. I bought it. And I'm hoping that it'll be your house, too." Paul stuck his hand in his pocket, pulled it out fist closed, then took one of her hands to his fist, which he opened, revealing a two-carat colorless cushion-cut diamond solitaire on a platinum band, the most beautiful engagement ring a girl could ever imagine.

Lily gasped.

Then Paul got down on one knee as he

knew men are to do at these sorts of times. "I know I'm leaving here in just a few weeks, but I'll be back, and I want to have you and this house to come back to. I love you and—"

"Yes!" she said, and she dropped down to her knees and embraced him and kissed him and they stayed like that on the front porch of their house for quite a long time.

A few weeks later

Just before sunrise, Lily lay in a big brand-new four-poster bed upstairs in the master bedroom of the house, asleep. In his uniform, hat under his arm, duffel bag by his side, Paul stood over her and watched her sleeping. He told himself to take the image of her like this into the far reaches of his mind. When he had done so, he took a deep breath, picked up his bag, turned, and very quietly left the room.

Downstairs, bag in hand, he opened the front door, walked out, and closed it slowly behind him. As he made his way across the front porch, suddenly the front door opened and Lily, in a bathrobe, ran out and threw herself into her husband's arms. He dropped the bag and his hat and embraced her.

After a moment, he kissed her, let her go, and walked down the front porch steps and down the walkway to a taxi waiting in the street.

Lily stood there in her robe, the sun rising, watching him go.

1945

Lily stood on her front porch looking out where the firework had been, remembering how she felt that day Paul left, different from how she felt now. She looked at her ring as she so often did. A symbol of her marriage, of course, it reminded her of Paul, and of the promise of the life that they would have. It was not only impressive in scale, it was, in all aspects of appraisal, near perfect, just like the house. Even though she hadn't known him very long, accepting the ring and the house and his proposal required little consideration. Proposals of marriage were quickly made and accepted all over the country at this time. Toccoa in particular was filled with bright-eyed young men in uniform, training at Camp Toccoa, who met, dated, and proposed to many of Lily's girlfriends. The world was at war and life decisions were made with impulse and passion.

The two weeks Lily and Paul had together after the wedding before he left for the war were wonderful. Despite what a girlfriend had told Lily, the nights were quite pleasant. Some nights were very pleasant.

Still, thinking about them, which was what she frequently found herself doing lately, left her with an imprecise though increasingly discernable sense of longing. And there was something about seeing that firework, something about how it made her feel, that seemed to focus this sense, sharpen it to the point where she couldn't ignore it, this deep feeling that . . . she was missing something or, more specifically, someone. Which of course, she told herself after a moment of consideration, made complete sense. After a lifetime in a small southern town hearing that the hungers of the body were sinful and corrupt and must be suppressed until holy matrimony, and then finally a taste of marriage, clumsy and rushed, and then three years and four months of ovulating and menstruating and ovulating, a cycle of desire and flow of no apparent use other than to mark the months spent sleeping alone, of course she felt a sense of longing to share her life. To share herself.

Indeed, except for this absence of her spouse, which in just a few days would no longer be an issue, by all standards she knew Lily's life was just the way it should be.

She sighed, running the evidence of this over in her head, but still, it did not entirely subdue the throbbing sense that something was . . . *What?* She reviewed the world again as though it were a hope chest, but all the articles were there. Yes, everything she wanted she had. Why then did she feel the way she did when she looked out at the firework? Why now this weight every time she let go breath? A warm current rushing into a cavity. A tidal pool in her soul. She couldn't explain it, but she could feel the drift, heavy and blue.

Rationally, her life was perfect. The facts were clear. But deep down, in a place where facts fell flat, a place where the firework touched, emotions churned.

Lily sighed and stared out at the western sky, squinting ever so slightly, recalling the poignant beauty of the firework. *From where did it come?* she wondered. *Who could have kindled such a powerful sky?*

JAKE RUSSO

The trajectory of the firework was just about right, thought Jake Russo, standing in the middle of a field just west of Toccoa. Now he could use that firing as a guide to calibrate and set many of the mortars he would use to shoot fireworks shells for the upcoming show.

Using a hand-bearing precision compass, Jake noted the exact direction of the firing and wrote it down in his small moleskin-covered journal. He made a few more notations regarding the approximate distance of the firing in relation to the direction and then shoved the worn journal back in a rear pocket. This field was going to be good, lots of space to work with.

Jake walked back to his big diesel freight truck parked near the edge of the grassy meadow, marched up the wood ramp, into the back, and located the mortars he needed. These were among the easiest to manage, simple black steel tubes, six inches wide, thirty-six inches long. The "bread and butter" of any solid pyrotechnics palette, they would be used to fire basic six-inch fireworks shells. In cabinets separated from the shells, the mortars were packed very tightly on wood shelves and secured with thick rubber banding so they could not knock together and create sparks.

Jake piled half a dozen of the steel mortar tubes on each shoulder, strode down the ramp, out into the field, and dumped them on the ground. This Georgia sun was intense, he thought.

Jake wore battered tank boots, snug blue jeans, and a denim workshirt over a tee. He took off his workshirt, used it to wipe the sweat from his brow, and tossed it down.

Then he picked up a shovel and started digging. Every single mortar used in the show, all 1,770 of them, had to be nearly entirely buried for stability. This would take hours of digging and hard manual labor. But Jake didn't mind. He liked this kind of work, especially when no one was shooting at him.

Just a few months ago, Jake was in fields and roadsides and backyards across Western Europe doing this same kind of work. Of course, his mortars weren't firing colorful pyrotechnics into the air. They were shooting high-explosive steel shells at German soldiers.

Right after his basic training in the spring of 1942, when the Army learned of Jake Russo's knowledge of and experience with fireworks, he was sent to the European Front and quickly made staff sergeant of a 60mm mortar section.

Jake literally grew up with fireworks. His father, Ernesto Russo, took the family's generations-old pyrotechnics secrets with him when he emigrated from Italy to America in 1911. Ernesto, soon joined by his brother, Federico, settled in Lawrence County, Pennsylvania, a thriving Italian community. Together they built Russo Fireworks. By the late 1930s, the Russos were one of the great American fireworks families, creating world-class pyrotechnics displays at state fairs, city-sponsored 4th of July celebrations, and even a presidential inauguration. All of that ended, of course, when the Japanese bombed Pearl Harbor and America was drawn into the war.

Despite that the Russos immediately converted to weapons manufacturing for the Army and were entirely committed to the American war effort, it was not a good time to be an Italian in America. Among numerous challenges at home, Ernesto, who spoke mostly Italian, was arrested by FBI agents as a "resident alien" and spent much of the war years in internment camps. However, staying true to the wishes of his father, this did not deter Jake from his commitment to duty when he was drafted by the Army.

From November 1942 to March 1943, Jake fought with the first wave of American forces in Algiers and Casablanca. In the fall of 1943, he served in the decisive battle for Salerno and for four months in 1944 fought the violent assault for Anzio. In 1945, during rest outside Rome, Jake met Lorena.

In his years in the fields and deserts and trenches, he had learned that it was best not to plan for tomorrow, but the widow had warmed something in him, something he dared trust. Nearly ten years older than him, she was raven haired, shapely, with deep sad eyes. He spoke enough Italian that they could get by. There was espresso in cracked porcelain demitasse cups, taken with biscuits while reading Thoreau aloud. A gift of a clean shirt made for him from wind-faded bedroom curtains that smelled of nebbiolo on the vine. In the pain of the destroyed land, she taught him about women, how to hold them, touch them, please them. Two days before his division headed for Germany, Jake thought about proposing to her, but all that ended with a click in a ruined vineyard, her smiling, walking toward him, and the sound of metal clasping metal. And in a portion of a second she was gone with an explosive and fiery shudder, bits of her bones and body torn and hurled through the smoke, cast about the ground before him like a rain of dark hail. Jake buried her in the vineyard and headed north.

On April 29, 1945, Jake Russo, with

troops from the 45th Infantry Division, fighting their way toward Munich, stumbled upon a place of barbed wire. In tattered wool pajamas, faded stripes, they peered out at him. Eyes in black sockets, in sunken bobbling skulls, reflecting the unimaginable, unspeakable horrors of the boneyards and furnaces behind them. Gaunt witnesses of the macabre, they stood and leaned and lay by the dozens and hundreds and thousands, their numbers overwhelming and terrifying and unhinging. Jake had no words to describe it. As much as war breaks a man's heart and damages his spirit, what Jake saw in that place called Dachau changed him.

Ten days later, on May 8, Berlin fell and Germany surrendered. Americans drank champagne and danced in the streets. GIs kissed girls in Times Square. And Jake came home. But home wasn't the same, not for Jake Russo. He wasn't the same. Despite what those in Lawrence County had read and thought they knew, they could never know what was now inside Jake Russo. He returned a stranger.

Jake stopped his digging, realizing that he'd buried all the mortar pipes he'd removed from the truck. His body told him that he was tired and hungry. He could rest, of course. He had plenty of time. But rest was something that Jake Russo did not welcome. Because when his body was at rest, his mind was not. And the places that his mind took him when unfettered were places he never cared to see again. Even in memory, they were terrible, unfathomable places. So Jake took comfort in labor, in constantly moving.

He considered the dozens of mortars already dug in, counted them, yanked out his pocket journal, and checked them off. Then he reviewed the list of remaining mortars for this show. It was time to start breaking out the bigger ones. He went back to the truck.

Loneliness really wasn't so bad, he often thought. There was a peace to it, and he cherished that. He had his fireworks and the simple blessings of each day. What more did a man truly need? Still, despite his best efforts, sometimes a feeling worked its way to mind, the desire for something greater, something beyond the rations and provisions on a soldier's checklist. Someday, he couldn't help thinking, it would be nice to have someone, to be close to a woman. Of course, that would most certainly require him to open up a part of himself that he feared was no longer there. And who could love someone like that? After all that he had seen, all that he had done, who could love what was left of Jake Russo?

So he remained determined to keep his feelings in check. Uttering his deepest thoughts only with rockets and mortars and shells bursting with stars.

TOCCOA

Lily drove her 1937 Packard down Doyle Street, right through the center of town. Her mother preferred that she drive Paul's company car, the Cadillac, especially for these kinds of outings. Letting such a fine automobile sit in a garage was un-American, Honey would assert. But Lily felt awkward in the massive Caddy, like she was wearing someone else's shoes. And it attracted too much attention when she drove it into town. That was, of course, one of the primary characteristics Honey admired about it. Still, even in her Packard, folks knew when Lily Davis was coming into town.

Many people out on the sidewalks looked up and waved when they saw the Packard cruising down Doyle. Lily found her smile, part of what she referred to as her "downtown face," and waved back. Coming to Doyle Street, the heart of Toccoa, always made Lily feel like one of the cheery mannequins in the display window of the Belk-Gallant department store, in front of where she was parking, everyone walking by, peering, assessing. She turned off the Packard and got out, taking in all the decorations that were beginning to go up for the 4th of July homecoming celebration.

This main street in downtown Toccoa looked like many other main streets in many small towns throughout the South. It was lined with two- and three-story brick buildings, storefronts at street level, apartments above. This was the economic center of all Stephens County.

When the Union soldiers retreated, leaving burned fields, mills, and cotton gins, the area was desolate. For several decades at the beginning of the century, King Cotton and "corn likker" provided primary sources of revenue for those who remained, mainly farmers and their families who lived off the land. In the 1930s, as good federally sponsored roads were built and modern industries grew, cotton and moonshine were generally, though not entirely, replaced by a wide variety of businesses in Toccoa, and more and more people started moving out of the countryside and into town.

It was particularly hot today, the midsummer heat rising off the asphalt on Doyle in hazy waves. Lily walked down the sidewalk, by the First National Bank of Toccoa, where her father was an adviser. She walked by the Barber Shoppe, where men played checkers and swapped information about the latest upgrades and modifications being made on their stock cars and made clandestine plans to race them on winding Appalachian roads. A few sipped small glasses of orange juice and "white lightning," the local shine from Gumlog, a storied hamlet a few miles away whose residents "drank their corn." Lily waved to a group of 4-H girls in uniform selling paper cups of sweet tea and mason jars of sourwood honey in front of Sosebee's Dixie Café. She walked by *The Toccoa Register*, Green's Department Store, and

Troup's Photo Service, which advertised in national farm magazines, bringing film from all around the country to be developed in Toccoa.

Just up the block, Lily saw a large group of townspeople tending to a massive vegetable field that had been cut into the lawn in front of the courthouse, just one of many Victory Gardens lining plots of city parks, backyards, and vacant lots throughout the city, where neighbors worked together to free up more food for the boys overseas and help feed their own community. The big forty-eight-star flag flapped high above the courthouse, its dome capped with locally mined Dahlonega gold leaf. The "rebel" Confederate flag, though not the legally sanctioned state flag, flew from the post in front of the courthouse, just above the community's sprawling Victory Garden.

There was a warmth to this town that was impossible not to feel on Doyle Street. However, along with the charms of Toccoa came a set of rules. Everyone knew them, and like them or not, they defined the world. "Our code of living" was how Lily heard people discuss them, particularly when something or someone threatened to break that code.

Passing her by were a gaggle of her mother's country club friends, cooling themselves with paper fans as they made their way down the sidewalk, several sipping sweet tea. With their languorous drawled greetings, they looked her up and down, taking in her hair and what she was wearing and where she was going, examining her like fingers running over Braille. More than accustomed to this sort of groping, she just kept her pleasant downtown face in place, submitted to the interaction, and then continued on her way.

Lily walked by a black man in uniform, an Army sergeant, a duffel bag beside him, turning the rusty handle on a drinking fountain, the COLORED sign hanging on a nail above slightly askew. He turned the handle as far as it would go, but nothing came out. The man was obviously passing though town and Lily wanted to tell him that as far as she could remember that fountain had never worked, but she did not. Lily saw him looking at the big fountain next to it, which was clearly working, the WHITES sign hanging over it, frosty water dribbling out of the head and puddling on the sidewalk. He nodded at Lily, an acknowledgment of her presence. Though he did not smile, it was, strangely, the deepest and most unfeigned greeting she had received on Doyle Street. She nodded back and, after a moment, he moved on.

As Lily pushed open the well-worn oak and screen door and entered Keener's, a small brass bell mounted above rang brightly.

"Lily! So nice to see you. How's your mother?"

"She's fine, Mrs. Keener. Thank you for asking," Lily responded to the owner of Keener's Produce & Market without any forethought, and began shopping.

The small plank-floored general store on the corner of Doyle and Pond Streets seemed to be overflowing with goods, compared to just a few months ago when rationing was at its peak and the shelves were nearly empty save for a few paltry items. Along with the usual boxes of Kraft Macaroni & Cheese dinners and tins of SPAM, a prime staple because it wasn't rationed as a meat, today there were also baskets of just-picked seasonal vegetables;

half-peck bags of pecans; smartly arranged rows of canned beans, stewing tomatoes, and chicken soups; sacks of flour and salt; even a little sugar. Treasures from a world returning. Cardboard tubes of M&M's, packs of Lucky Strikes, and quarts of hand-cranked fresh peach ice cream were also in stock behind the counter.

Many other customers happily shopped as well, but it was Lily who got the most attention from the proprietor. During the early 1930s, when many people were struggling to get back on their feet, Lily's father had loaned Mr. Keener fifteen thousand dollars so he could keep the market open. No collateral, just Mr. Keener's word that he would pay it back, which he did. Ever since, the Keeners, like many folks in Toccoa, felt a deep sense of indebtedness to the Davises, which went far beyond an initial loan. Lily was often the recipient of their gratitude.

"Now you be sure to tell your mother I was asking about her," said Mrs. Keener.

"Of course I will."

Lily had this kind of conversation—women of the town asking about her mother—so frequently that her responses came as involuntarily as breathing. Ever since she could remember, people asked her, first and foremost, about her parents, her mother in particular. On more than one occasion Lily came very close to screaming out at a church or a bus stop or a hardware store: *My mother?! My mother?! My mother is unyielding and demanding and nothing I do ever seems to please her! That is how she is!*

"Good afternoon, Lily," said Evelyn Tabor, whose husband owned Tabor Motor Company and who was shopping with her eight-year-old, Mary.

"Good afternoon, Mrs. Tabor."

"Does your mother have a big party planned at Holly Hills for Paul's homecoming?"

Lily felt Evelyn Tabor looking her over with the same kind of shameless scrutiny that one uses to examine a melon. Lily just smiled, gracefully tucking a stray strand of hair behind her ear.

"You know my mother, she'd never miss an opportunity for a party."

Lily made her way through the aisles of the small market, smiling a greeting to several others and placing a few items in her basket: summer squash, okra, a small slab of sweet butter, a box of saltine crackers—*oh, how she loved warm buttered saltines!*—a quart of ice cream, and a pack of teaberry gum. Heading for the register, Lily looked in her basket and could hear her mother's criticism about her whimsical purchases. Visibly rolling her eyes a bit, she headed for the register.

Behind the counter, a young boy with dark hair whom Lily had never seen before unpacked onions from a wooden crate.

"Hello," she said with a sweet and genuine smile. "What's your name?"

He just looked at her for a long moment and then returned to his task.

"Lily," Mrs. Keener called Lily over to the register.

"For the homecoming," Mrs. Keener said conspiratorially as she produced a bottle of fine red wine.

"Mrs. Keener, that is too generous, I can't—"

"I insist."

Mrs. Keener popped open a couple of brown paper "S.O.S." sacks, the smart "self-opening sacks" that Keener's had been giving its customers for nearly a decade now. She slipped the bottle into one of the sacks along with Lily's groceries.

This was an extravagant gift and Lily continued to resist, but her expressions were nominal, polite at best. She was accustomed to people giving her things like this. Her mother taught her long ago that the act of accepting these kinds of things required its own kind of graciousness, even if she knew full well that people were simply trying to curry favor with her family. This was how things were in Toccoa, Georgia. And as much as they often drove Lily to silent, desperate madness, she also understood that they gave her, and everyone for that matter, a sense of place, a sense of belonging. She was Lily Davis Woodward, daughter of Honey and Walter Davis, wife of Paul Woodward. She had a place in the world, and her children would, too.

"Thank you, Mrs. Keener. You are so kind. I will be sure to pass on your regards to my mother."

Mrs. Keener smiled, quite pleased with that response, and moved on to help another customer.

The boy with the dark hair just looked at Lily, blinking, pondering, as if he knew something that she did not. After a moment, she turned away from him and started to leave the store, mindlessly holding grocery bags in her arms.

Lily saw something outside, stopped, and turned. "Do you have any Coca-Cola, Mrs. Keener?"

"Well, not officially in stock. But for you, Lily, I think we can find a Co-Cola."

Mrs. Keener grinned over her big teeth, yellow as stable straw, reached below the counter, and produced a soft drink bottle, icy and dripping, popped off the metal cap, and handed the Coke to Lily. She could smell the sweet cassia and caramel in the fizzing carbonation.

"Thanks."

Coke and sacks in hand, Lily walked out, the brass bell ringing over her.

On the sidewalk, Lily approached the sergeant she'd seen at the water fountain. He sat quietly on a bench under the spotty shade of an elm, uniform drenched through with sweat, duffel bag at his feet.

"Good afternoon, Sergeant," said Lily.

"Ma'am."

"I wonder if you might help me carry these heavy bags to my car over there."

He stood up immediately. "Would be my pleasure."

"I don't have much to offer you, though," Lily said. "Except this Coke."

"That is not necessary."

"I insist."

He considered her for a moment. "Well, thank you."

He accepted the soft drink, took a big, deep swallow, and then took her bags. Immediately feeling how light they were, he knew that she did not need help carrying them. And she could see that he knew this. They exchanged a smile of respect and understanding.

"It's a lovely day, don't you think?" said Lily.

"Yes, I do. A lovely day," the sergeant replied.

They walked together, side by side, across Doyle Street toward Lily's car. Many people they passed smiled politely.

Mrs. Keener watched through the window of her store as her Coke was given away. A Davis or not, Mrs. Keener thought, there was something going on with Lily that went much further than the expression she carried on her face. Yes, Lily Davis Woodward was a much more complicated girl than most folks knew. And if she wasn't careful, one day that was going to get her into trouble.

A CHANCE MEETING

Heading north, Lily drove the Packard down Currahee Street to the east of town until it became Highway 123. After a few miles, she pulled off onto Owl Swamp Road, a rural two-lane that wound through pine forest north of town. It was late afternoon but still wickedly hot, and even with the windows fully rolled down, Lily perspired profusely. But she didn't care. She loved the forest around her, verdant and hushed, the warm, wet breeze carelessly whipping her hair. Lily unfastened the top buttons of her nice summer dress, letting the wind meet her damp skin.

Nearly halfway back to her house, as she was crossing Prather Bridge, another jarring *boom* shocked her from her heat-induced reverie—but this one was much louder than the one she'd heard earlier with Honey. It shook the car.

Lily pulled over to the side of the road and saw a silver trail of light fly up into the sky. Mesmerized, she opened the door, leaving the engine running, got out of the car, and walked toward the climbing sparkling light. It seemed to be very close, just over her head. She could hear it whistling as it climbed above the grassy field into which she was walking.

Then, *boom-boom*, even louder again, and the trail exploded into thousands of beads of light, each one shooting out on its own dazzling trajectory, filling the entire blue and white canvas over the meadow with shimmering silver tinsel. Lily just stood in the field, looking straight up, slowly, reflexively, turning, as the firework continued expanding, engraving the sky.

Lily had never seen anything like this. It was beautiful and powerful and magical. She was so fascinated, so taken by what she saw, that she didn't hear the voice that was calling out to her: *"Look out! Get away from there!"*

When she finally heard the voice, registered the alarm it was trying to impart, and looked around to see from where it was coming and what exactly it meant, suddenly a young man in boots, jeans, and a dirty white T-shirt tackled her, pulled her to the ground, and lay on top of her, forcefully covering her with his entire body.

Before Lily could even find a breath to scream, she saw the pieces of smoking debris from the firework landing all around them. Some of the pieces missed them by inches.

Realizing what was happening, she lay still. His cheek pressed to hers, his hands cupped around her face, his chest on her back, his hips on hers, he lay still.

The last of the debris fell. But Lily and the man continued to lie there, frozen, for a long moment. Until, slowly, gingerly, he rolled off her.

"Didn't anyone ever teach you not to stand under fireworks?"

Lily lifted her face off the ground and

took in Jake Russo. Though he was clearly just a few years older than her, he had a quiet, knowing sense about him that was much worldlier than usual in someone his age. His eyes were dark and mature. His tousled hair and three-day beard were ink black. While visibly lean, his body felt muscular, not simply taut, like a young man's, but hard, presumably from use.

He reached out a hand to her. She took it and he helped her up, never taking his eyes off her. *What is a beautiful girl like this doing in the middle of a field in the middle of Georgia?* he wondered.

"I feel like an idiot," she said.

"You've got a pebble stuck to your chin."

Lily swatted at her face.

"I suppose I should say 'thank you.'"

"I suppose I should say 'don't worry about it.'"

Jake reached out to her and removed a tiny stone that was pressed to her face. Lily considered him as he did this. He smelled of sweat and earth and black powder. And now she did, too. It was animal. Visceral. Her father smelled this way when he returned from extended camping trips in the Appalachians when she was a child.

Trying to get her bearings, Lily looked around, tossing some stray strands of hair from her face. As she looked up, light refracted in the tawny trails still lingering, like viscous nectar from a great tupelo comb hewn and oozing over the clouds.

Not too far from where they were standing, Lily saw the freight truck and several rows of buried mortars in the field.

"That your truck over there?"

"That's mine."

"So you must be the pyrotechnics man."

"That would be me."

There was a moment of silence. Jake just looked at her, and she let him. She felt him studying her, considering her. This sort of thing would usually compel her to make some sweet small talk about the weather or an upcoming party and gracefully move the moment along, but she didn't. She just let this be, surprised by how natural it felt.

"What are you doing out here?" he finally said.

"I was just driving by and I saw the firework, your firework, and I thought it was amazing, and I wanted to watch it." Without meaning to, Lily let words just fall out of her. She felt so uncharacteristically clumsy and rationalized that she must be a little dizzy from being tackled.

Without realizing it, Jake smiled, in a way he hadn't for a long time. There was something about her, beautiful, yes, but also something . . . confident, unapologetic eyes, like blue sapphires, like cobalt, both profound and elemental, a proper dress improperly buttoned, she was refined but bold . . . so many things, actually, that made her so hard to stop looking at.

Feeling the sun on his neck, beads of perspiration rolling down his cheek, Jake just stood there in the stillness and the heat, legs firmly astride, one knee slightly bent, arms down, palms a little forward as if ready to receive something, maintaining his controlled breathing and his constant gaze at her, afraid that if he broke it and looked away, or even just moved from his stance, she'd see how nervous her beauty and being this near her was actually making him. Finally, he wiped his forehead with the back of his wrist.

"You're bleeding," he said, squinting and pointing to her scraped knee.

"Oh," whispered Lily, embarrassed that

she hadn't even noticed how much it really hurt until just now.

"That has to be cleaned." He hooked a finger into a belt loop on his jeans and again just watched her.

"Well, I'm just all out of sorts this afternoon." She tried to wipe some dirt off the wound but only made things worse. "Ow!" This did have to be cleaned.

"I have some antiseptic in the truck. Why don't you hobble on over to it," he said, noticing her car off on the side of the road. "I'll turn off your engine and be right there."

"You're too kind. But I feel like I've already caused you enough trouble."

"No trouble."

Lily looked at him for a moment and, without further reflection, decided to accept help from this stranger. "Thank you. I'm Lily. Lily Davis Woodward."

"Jake Russo."

"Pleased to meet you, Jake Russo."

Jake nodded and began to head for Lily's car. Then he stopped.

"By the way, what you said about fireworks, I think they're amazing, too."

Having no idea how much that comment made her like him, Jake quickly marched off, the late afternoon sun before him bronzing everything it touched.

CANDLELIGHT AND MAGIC

I know I'd seen them even earlier, but the first one I vividly remember was when I was three," said Jake.

"You remember that far back?"

"Like it was yesterday."

Lily grimaced a bit. She sat on the edge of the truck ramp. Legs dangling. Dress pulled up mid-thigh. Jake stood and wiped dirt and tiny rocks from her knee using gauze moistened with a strong distillate of witch hazel. She was also barefoot because, unlike his rubberized tank boots, her jute-soled espadrilles could create static electricity, not something you wanted on a fireworks truck.

"It was a twenty-four-inch multibreak 'weeping willow,'" Jake continued as he gently tended to her knee. "Like the one you saw in the field, only bigger."

"Bigger?"

"See those shells over there?" Jake pointed to several large fireworks shells secured on a grounded metal shelf in the back of the truck. "Those are thirty-sixers, three feet in diameter. One of my family's specialties. My father really mastered them. Each one takes several hours to make, and each one makes the night brighter than noon in July."

Lily took in the sight of all the shells secured in the back of the truck. About ten feet away from the truck, on a large folding wooden table, were several gallon-sized heavy cardboard containers filled with fine powders, each a different color; another container of long black-powdered cord, presumably fuses; and a stack of heavy brown paper. A few fireworks shells sat on the table in various stages of construction and repair. Lily was enthralled. It was like peering into a sorcerer's workshop.

"All that time and work for something that lasts a few seconds," she said.

"A moment in the sky, forever in the heart." Jake smiled, surprising himself again.

Lily nodded, understanding entirely. "That's nice."

"That's my father. Well, the English version. What he always said was more like *'in cielo per un attimo, in testa per una vita, e nel cuore per sempre.'*"

Lily didn't realize how lyrical, how romantic, really, Italian sounded. It was, after all, the language of the enemy, and so one didn't hear it very often. Certainly not the way Jake Russo made it sound.

She continued listening to him talk, passionately about fireworks, vaguely about himself. She was intrigued by both what he was saying and how he was saying it. He used words comfortably but sparingly; he was at ease but measured. Such a fascinating bundle of contradictions, this man. He looked tough but spoke thoughtfully. He was a laborer, and an artist. His hands were rough; his touch, gentle, tender. He was complicated, Jake Russo, so different from the boys and men in Toccoa whose nature and needs were so readily apparent.

Lily looked up and saw an old pickup driving down Owl Swamp Road. It slowed when the driver saw her Packard parked by the side of the road and then sped up and continued. *Was that the Browns' pickup?* Lily wondered. She wasn't sure. Had they recognized her car? If it was the Browns, probably not. They'd recognize Paul's Cadillac but not the Packard. But why did she care? She wasn't doing anything wrong. Of course, her neighbors might not see it that way. Yes, Lily Davis in a dirty dress, alone with a boy in a field; some would certainly say that flew in the face of the old Toccoa code of living.

"Lived in Georgia all your life?" Jake said, blowing on her knee to help the excess alcohol evaporate.

The sensation of his breath lingering on her skin distracted her from her previous thoughts. "That obvious?" she said.

"It's your accent, mostly." Jake had served with men from all over the United States. Long days spent in muddy foxholes with men from South Carolina, Tennessee, and Georgia had made him quite expert in the subtleties of various regional accents.

"Yes, all my life."

"Your husband from the area, too?"

"Paul is from Gainesville, just north of Atlanta." She had seen him notice her ring and knew he was asking about more than where Paul was from. "He's been stationed overseas. He's returning in a few days."

Jake expertly secured a small square of gauze to the scrape with some white surgical tape. "There. All set."

"You've done this before."

"That obvious?"

Lily smiled. "Thank you." She pushed her dress down, stood, and hopped off the truck ramp. She slid into her sandals. "I wish I could do something to return the favor."

"No need. Honestly, it's been nice just to talk for a little while. I've really enjoyed it."

"I'll bring you a pie. A pecan pie. That's what we do in Toccoa. Baking. Lots of baking, usually with nuts. Where are you staying?"

"The Auxiliary has a room for me. But I'll most likely stay out here. I've got all my gear, everything I need, and I prefer it."

Jake realized that Lily was shaking her head. "You okay?" he said.

"I'm just remembering, I've got a trunk full of ice cream and butter."

"In this heat?"

Lily realized her groceries were probably ruined. "I'm not usually like this. Really. I don't know what's wrong with me today."

Jake laughed. Increasingly certain that he was seeing a part of this young woman that very few ever saw. A part she kept carefully hidden, maybe even from herself. And he liked it. He liked it a lot.

Jake had learned during his time at war that there are moments in one's life, critical moments, small moments, passing flutters of a second, in which decisions are made and actions taken, perhaps the slightest of offers extended, that at the time on the surface seem simple and transparent but upon consideration or reflection are proven to be instants that can change the course of everything.

As she stood there in her sandals in that field, smiling comfortably at him, an evening breeze kicking up, tossing her hair, rippling her dress, the feel of the skin of her leg rooted in his mind like a lovely haunting melody, growing louder and more resolute each time he tried to forget it, on a level that he was not wholly aware of at the time, this was one of those moments. It could have ended there, Jake knew. There was nothing else between them, and the last thing he needed was a complication. He was decidedly avoiding such things in his life. That was one of the main reasons he was here, after all. *Say good-bye, wish her well, do the show, and move on to the next town*, he told his conscious self.

But after several years of living by his gut, literally surviving on what it directed him to do, he once again found himself acting on that core instinct. "Would you like to stay for dinner?" he asked. "I don't have much. But there's some risotto, and I'm not entirely bad with my little camp stove. And I suppose we could have ice-cream soup for dessert."

Lily was a little taken aback by the offer. But she continued standing there. "You save my life, you bandage my knee, I can't have you feed me, too. The Ladies Auxiliary will throw me out of Toccoa for being such a poor southern hostess."

"So we won't tell them."

How long had it been since she'd been invited to dinner, to anything, by someone besides her parents or someone who was connected to her parents? Dinner. More time with this man. Yes. That was exactly what she wanted. Was it okay? Was it proper? Was it right? She didn't know. But she was in the middle of a grassy field and the sun was going down and Jake Russo had been nothing but nice and kind and interesting, and all she knew for sure was that she wanted more. And that, that certainty, felt right.

"I can stay."

Sunset on the outskirts of Toccoa on the last night of June 1945 was a glorious affair. The air was warm and still. Fireflies came to life, first one by one, then by the dozens. A bullfrog bellowed lazily from the nearby stream. Jake retrieved several large candles, which he used behind the scenes at his shows, and lit them. He placed one on a small table, used to lay out his notes and directions during shows and now set with tin plates for dinner. He placed several more candles on the ground nearby and a couple more near the camp stove, where risotto and canned chicken broth simmered slowly in a cast-iron pan.

"Well, you sure picked a beautiful place to live your entire life," said Jake.

"Yes. I think most of the time I take it for granted. A night like this really makes you appreciate it."

Lily felt as though all her senses were heightened. The heady smell of the browning Italian rice in the field, the chorus of crickets singing their night song, and this man, lithely moving in and out of the shadows like a magician; there was something about the composite of the experiences that made her feel more like she was watching her life instead of living it.

As suspected, the ice cream and butter had melted. After throwing away the bag that contained them, Lily consolidated the remaining groceries and transferred them to the other bag, which she had brought with her from the car. Using a very sharp utility knife, she cut the squash into slices. Jake moved up next to her, poured more broth from an open can into the risotto, and slowly stirred.

"So your family has been making fireworks for a long time."

"Yes, they have."

"I know. You told me. I was making a

statement, a leading statement." Jake just looked at her. "As in leading you to telling me a little more about yourself. It's a polite way of asking."

"A statement instead of a question." Jake chewed on this notion.

"We're very big on that sort of thing in Georgia."

"Being polite?"

"And nosy."

Jake smiled and nodded. "Sorry. I'm not accustomed to too much politeness. Or talking much about myself."

"It's okay."

They stood next to each other, continuing to prepare the meal. "It really is a beautiful night," Lily said, retreating to the well-trodden path of surface-level conversation.

Jake sighed a little, trying to remember what was once so natural. "My family made pyrotechnics for hundreds of years. In Teano, a small village near Naples. My father and his brother brought the trade with them when they settled in New Castle, in Pennsylvania. And now that the war is over, we're at it again."

"And *you're* at it again."

"That sounds suspiciously like a statement."

"You're getting good at this."

Jake looked at her grinning at him playfully. He did like talking to her. Very much. "I've always loved fireworks. While some kids were learning how to throw a curveball I was learning how to mix saltpeter and sulfur. I always assumed I'd work in the family business. And now that the war is over, I have that opportunity. In the next few weeks I'll be going to Nantucket, Chicago, and Boulder. In the fall, San Francisco and Taos. We're even getting calls from Brazil and Canada. A lot of them in fact. People are calling from all over the world now that the war is ending."

"Isn't this a lot of work for one man?"

"I can handle it."

"That's not what I asked."

"At the bigger venues, I'll pick up local help if I need it. My family can send the shells to locations if necessary. But I'm pretty self-sufficient. Three years in the Army will do that to you."

Lily took in this new piece of information. "When did you get back?"

"Five weeks ago."

"You're a man who doesn't like to sit still."

Jake tasted the risotto, added a little salt and then a bit more broth. "So you're born and raised in Toccoa."

"Yes," said Lily, recognizing that he was changing the subject. "But you already know that."

"Yes, I do."

"Is that a leading statement, sir?"

"Why, I believe it is, ma'am."

Lily shot him a smile and took in the earthy smell of the risotto. "Would you like some wine?"

She pulled the bottle Mrs. Keener had given her out of the bag.

"Well, you're a handy girl to find in a field."

Candlelight coalesced with moonlight, and in the strange and wonderful glow Lily and Jake sat at the small table in the middle of the field and dined. The magic of the night put into relief for both how long it had been since either had shared the intimacy of a meal like this. And in both this gave rise to all sorts of strong and unanticipated emotions.

Lily took a bite of the risotto with squash, closing her eyes and reveling in how good it tasted. She was amazed at how pleasurable something so simple could be. "Uhm . . . This is so . . . oh . . . what's the word? . . . otherworldly."

"Otherworldly?"

"Yes, as in from a world not of Toccoa."

Unable to contain his smile, Jake was pleased by how much she was openly enjoying the meal. "People have developed so many rules about cooking risotto. I've seen fistfights break out in kitchens. What kind of rice, how much broth, what kind of spoon to use, which direction to stir. It's so silly. At the end of the day it's a peasant dish made and eaten for centuries in settings pretty much like this. As long as you have *vialone nano*, a good rice, and *buono compagnia*, good company, and you trust your instincts, it always turns out perfect. Although what my mother does with it is maybe a step beyond."

She took another bite. As much as she enjoyed eating it, Jake enjoyed watching her.

"Uh, I can't believe I've never had this before," Lily mused.

"Yeah, spaghetti is as close as most Americans get to Italian food."

"Well, you've completely ruined me for spaghetti."

"I'll leave you the rest of the bag."

"I don't think it'll turn out the same. I'm a famously poor cook."

"I don't believe that for two seconds."

"Oh, just ask *my* mother."

"When I was a kid, fireworks always seemed like such a mystery. My father used to say to me, 'If you love them, you can make them.' Cooking is just like making fireworks. After you learn the recipes, you try to forget them and you trust your instincts—you give in to them. You take a little of this, and a little of that, separate and distinct sensations, and you mix it all together and, *boom*, you create something wonderful that didn't exist before."

He looked at her for a long moment. "I've seen you eat. I've seen what fireworks do to you. I bet you're an amazing cook."

For some reason, she felt the blood rush to her face. She wondered if he could see it in the candlelight.

Jake poured more wine for Lily into a Duralex bistro tumbler made from tempered French glass. Then he poured more into his own. Although she was aware of a dull, distant sense of guilt about not sharing the fine 1937 Haut Brion with Paul as Mrs. Keener had intended, Lily felt certain she would have more regret about not opening the bottle here and now. In this place, with this meal, with this man who had prepared it.

"Sounds like a very wise man, your father."

"Yeah."

Lily raised her glass. *"'A moment in the sky, forever in the heart.'"*

Jake touched his glass to hers and drank.

"My father camped a lot when I was growing up," Lily said in a far-off voice. "Usually with men from his company, but one time—I remember it now like it was yesterday—one time, he took me with him. Just me. And we sat outside at night, like this, and we ate brook trout, which we'd caught that day and roasted over an open fire on a piece of cedarwood. We were right up there, right on that ridge." Lily pointed to the northwest, to the peak of Currahee Mountain, and then took a bite of risotto and a sip of the Haut Brion, a sublime combination.

"You know that spot well."

"I see it most every day."

Jake could hear in her voice how special this place was to her. "Sounds like your father is a busy man."

"After law school he went to work for Coke. He's head of international marketing. He was mayor of Toccoa when I was in junior high. Now he's state senator for our district. But his biggest job is being married to my mother. She's the one who really runs things around here. She's had us all working overtime lately getting ready for Paul's return."

"Your husband."

"Yes."

"How long has he been away?"

"About the same amount of time you were gone. Three years."

"That's a long time."

Lily took a moment, looked off, and then came back to him and met his eyes. "Do you think you've changed, Jake? Since you were gone? Do you think you've changed?"

"I think people at home think I've changed," he responded in his measured way.

"You sound like you don't agree with them."

Jake knew precisely what she was asking, her concerns about what the man she married would be like, though he was not exactly sure what she wanted to hear. He thought about his response for a long moment.

"Have you heard from your husband?"

"I've gotten a postcard or a letter from him at least every other week."

"That's a lot."

"I've spoken to him on the phone seven times. Hawaii, Philippines, New Guinea, Morocco, England, Italy, Germany."

"He must be a high-ranking officer."

"Paul is a business executive with Coke. He provides support services for the armed forces. If you ever drank a Coca-Cola overseas, I'm sure Paul had a hand in setting it up."

"Ah, he's a 'Coke colonel,'" said Jake, referencing the nickname given to the Coke men by GIs. Jake had certainly had his share of Cokes while overseas. He'd been amazed how quickly the carbonated beverages often showed up in the most forsaken places, sometimes just hours after the fighting had stopped. After Jake fought to secure the beaches in North Africa, among the heavy weapons and provisions brought ashore by military craft was all the equipment and materials necessary to construct and run a complete Coca-Cola bottling plant, everything necessary to supply the troops with bottles of the carbonated beverage. The images of body bags being loaded onto boats that were simultaneously unloading big canisters of Coke syrup and crate upon crate of those empty famously contoured glass bottles was something Jake would never forget.

A lot of American companies were sending their products to the men on the front lines. But the "Coke colonels," Jake had noticed, worked hard not only to keep Allied soldiers sated but also to keep the company's sixty-four overseas bottling plants operating throughout the war, especially those in Coke's biggest European market, Germany.

Jake found it perplexing and strange that an American company seemed at once both patriotic and traitorous, but he had learned that despite what many thought, nothing in war is ever black and white. This was one of the reasons it was so hard to talk to people back home in Lawrence County who saw it that way.

Did he think her husband had changed? Did he think *he* had changed?

How could he explain what it was like to look into the eyes of a man trying his hardest to kill you? The bright flash from the rifle, the slow-motion terror of shell casings popping, one, two, three, and lead slugs flying by so close you can feel the hot air on your cheek. And then watching up close as the slugs hit the man next to you? How could Jake explain? There were no words to convey these feelings, no pictures to do them justice.

Jake took the night air deep into his lungs, his eyes refocusing on her. "I think the whole world has changed," he said. "Those of us overseas. And those at home. Everyone. Everything. And the thing is, not everyone knows it yet."

Though she wasn't sure exactly why, Lily felt herself tearing up. She turned away from him and willed the tears to stop. What he said really struck a chord with her. On the outside, everything was as it always was. The world seemed to stand still in

Toccoa, and when she looked around and took stock of her life everything was as it should be. But on the inside, buried deep, she knew there'd been a shift of some sort. That warm current again. It wasn't something she was consciously aware of, like oxygen in the air, but every time she breathed in she knew it to be there, knew it was in the composite coursing throughout her body. It was subtle, indistinct, but nonetheless profound.

As the emotions washed over Lily, churning inside her, she realized that seeing the firework from her front porch earlier in the day had made her aware of something that had been hidden away inside, shoved and stacked into some secret niche. Meeting this man, being out here with him tonight, it was all coming to the surface, this deep restlessness, and it was stirring her in unexpected ways.

She didn't know if Paul would be different, but the honest fact was, *she* felt different than she did three years ago. How much was due to the world changing and how much was her she didn't know. But the drift was present and palpable.

The conversation could have gone in

one of several directions. Lily chose one. "So do you have a girl, Jake Russo?"

"I have my work."

"And that's all?"

"That's enough."

"I think I'd get lonesome traveling around by myself," she said gently.

"I think I'd get lonesome living with my spouse gone for three years," he said even more gently.

"He'll be back in a few days."

"And then—?"

"And then . . ." She trailed off, looking away from him. It was pretty bold for him to question her like this, something to which she was quite unaccustomed. No one ever spoke to her with this kind of frankness and sincere interest. And she never spoke back to anyone this way. Still, for some reason, she wanted to be as honest with him as she possibly could be.

She reconnected with his eyes. "And then, I begin my life. We'll start a family. He'll build his career."

"Sounds like a plan."

"Yes. I'm part of something. I have a house, a husband, a community. My life is . . . planned." Lily meant for this to sound effortless, obvious, just as it did when she spoke to people at church or Keener's Market. But somehow as she was talking to him, it didn't come out that way. She felt him looking not just into her eyes but also beyond them, as though he could see into her. "And yours?"

"My plan? My plan is my fireworks."

"And then—?"

"Then?"

"I mean, how long are you going to be on the road?"

"I don't know. Guess I don't have much of a plan, least not beyond what's in my truck."

They shared a smile, the sad, whimsical smile of two strangers who shared a moment of truth the way only strangers can. Then they continued eating the risotto and drinking the Bordeaux, each enjoying the experience, however transitory, of being close to another person after so long a time spent alone.

After lingering over the remaining wine, Lily cleared the table while Jake drew more water from the stream. Together they washed the tin plates and forks in a metal bucket of soapy water and then rinsed them clean.

Jake scooped several fistfuls of oily dark-roasted coffee beans from a large burlap sack, dropped them in an old portable coffee mill, and carefully hand-ground them to a fine powder. He produced an aluminum *moka* espresso pot, black Bakelite handled, filled the lower chamber with water, packed the middle filter with the ground coffee and inserted it into the lower chamber, and screwed the upper vessel tightly onto the lower chamber base. Then he placed the *moka* pot on the lit camp stove. Having never seen a device like this before, so simple but so precise, Lily watched in silent fascination. After a few minutes, as steam and boiling water rose forcefully from the lower chamber through the coffee and collected in the top vessel, the *moka* pot began to gurgle. Listening exactingly to the sound, Jake removed the device from the heat at a particular moment. Then he poured ample servings of the rich espresso into two clean Duralex glasses.

He unfolded two field chairs and set a couple of the candles in front of them. He opened the door to the cab of the truck and tuned the radio to WHAS, a Clear Channel station from Louisville whose big band programming could be heard throughout the eastern part of the country at night.

Lily and Jake sat together peacefully, a little talked out, and sipped their coffee as Helen Forrest sang "Bewitched, Bothered and Bewildered." It was strangely moving, ethereal, the haunting ballad wafting out into the moonlit field.

Jake took out his pocket journal, its brown cover supple and felted as a club chair, and a small molar-marked pencil that he kept stuck in the pages.

"I have an idea about something I want to flesh out a little. Do you mind?"

"Not at all."

After days in the trenches with nothing to do but think and wait, Jake had gotten in the habit of always having something with him in which to write. In Italy, he had picked up several of these small moleskin journals, which bent and molded very comfortably in a rear pocket.

Lily assumed he was writing a poem or a story, his diary perhaps. She didn't ask.

This seemed a natural part of his rhythm, something he often did. If he wanted to share it, he would. She just leaned back in her chair. There was something deeply comforting about him writing next to her. For one thing, it gave her permission to take in the night and the music and swim in her own thoughts. She'd never had coffee this good before, didn't even know it could be like this. Thin reddish creamlike foam floating on an oily black syrup. And she'd certainly never seen someone make it with such care. Her father was demanding about his coffee. Rationing be damned, there was always Stewarts coffee in the Davis household. But as far as Lily could remember, she had never once seen her father make it. As far as she could remember, she had never seen anyone, male or female, make coffee this passionately. That was the word for Jake. "Passionate." Everything Jake Russo did, everything about him, was like that. Fireworks, risotto, coffee, the music he chose, the words he used, the way he moved in those jeans, keenly, purposefully. His touch on her leg, the way he blew on her knee. The girls in town would be so attracted to him.

Or would they? Would they understand him and see what she saw? Or would they think he was just quiet and strange and lonely? He was all that, of course. But those things only contributed to what she found so interesting about him. He was certainly very different from most of the boys she grew up with and knew.

Where did he sleep? In the small overhead cab of the truck or outside, under the stars? She had seen sleeping bags in the back of the truck. Yes, there was more than one. What did that mean? Who was the other one for? Her mind wandered freely.

He would meet someone. Eventually. And in ways big and small that other woman would receive the totality of his nature, his intensity, sensitivity, ability to focus all of himself on a woman as though understanding her and knowing her and feeling what she was feeling was the most important thing there was. That he was going to sweep a woman away, Lily was certain, and it made her content inside to know and think about, that he would not be alone, and that someone else would be so deeply connected to him and share her life with him, but the more Lily knew it, the more it also made her a little sad. More than a little, perhaps. It was wrong to feel that way, she told herself. But there it was. There it was. As plain as the waxing gibbous moon glowing above them. There it was, clear as that.

It seemed to have gotten warmer, stickier. Perhaps it was the coffee. Lily felt the slip under her dress clinging to her body. She tugged on the top of her dress, to let a little more air onto her skin. As she moved her head to inspect the top buttons, something caught her eye in the southwestern sky. She pointed to it.

"A shooting star!"

Though Jake was looking up, he just stared, not seeing it, and it was gone.

"It was right there, where you were looking, just under Cassiopeia."

"I love the stars, I really do. But, honestly, when I look up like this, I don't see them."

"What do you see?"

"A blank slate."

Lily looked up, then back at him, not understanding.

Jake thought for a moment, then he handed her his notebook. "Here. This is what I see."

She looked at it, confused, and started reading what looked like a recipe of some sort.

"'Sixty-five ounces BP plus fifty ounces magnesium.'"

"Sixty-five ounces of black powder," Jake explained. "It's a precise mixture of sulphur, charcoal, and saltpeter. That's the lifting charge. A big one. It'll give a strong *bang* to kick things off. The shell pops out of the mortar, flies high and fast into the sky, five thousand meters up, leaving a comet trail of flittering white sparks. That's the magnesium."

Lily was fascinated, realizing that she was looking at the handwritten formula for a firework. She continued reading. "'Ten BP, one hundred stars—strontium carbonate.'"

"First break explodes, *boom*, red stars shoot across the sky in a perfect sphere twenty-five hundred meters across."

"'Twenty BP, two hundred stars—barium chlorate.'"

"Second break, *boom*, green stars, like jade and emeralds, twice as many, five thousand meters across."

"'Thirty BP, three hundred stars—sodium oxalate, five-sec. fuse . . .'"

"There's a time-delay fuse, three, two, one, third break, *boom!* three hundred yellow stars . . . it's like sunlight piercing the heavens."

"'Fifty ounces aluminum.'"

"And a quick flash of light, for punctuation, as the stars flare out and fade."

They sat there a moment, looking up at the sky, envisioning it.

Strontium, barium, sodium oxalate; it was a poem, Lily thought. Its words, chemistry; its paper, sky. "It's beautiful," she finally said.

"A triple-break chrysanthemum. Yeah, that would be something."

Jake went on to explain that nearly all the fireworks were premade by hand in Lawrence County, in the traditional style, as they had been for centuries. Jake described in heartfelt detail the way his family made fireworks on their property in the northern rural part of the county, in New Castle. There were numerous small concrete buildings with grounded corrugated iron roofs, called magazines, scattered about one hundred feet from each other so that if one exploded, the others would be spared. Some of the small buildings were entirely packed to the roof with finished fireworks shells of every size and shape imaginable. Others stored vats of raw explosives and chemical powders. And others were used for manufacturing. In these production buildings, Jake's family members and several close friends from Italy and their families would assemble fireworks shells. They would mix and bake special chemical batters, from which they would cut small stars that looked just like holiday cookies. They would create colorful compounds from secret substances, which would be packed into the outer layers of multibreak shells. They would produce and pack entire pyrotechnics shows of all sizes and all ranges of spectacle to be shipped to destinations all over the globe. A dozen friends and family members, in a small concrete room, sitting and laughing and working together, creating magic to delight people far away whom they would never meet but to whom they would always be connected. This was how it was always done. This was how it was still done.

While on the road, Jake simply set up the mortars, loaded the preconstructed shells, planned out the fine points of a specific show in his journal, and then fired it in the right sequence. But he also liked to do some design work while he traveled. He liked to write and dream and experiment a little. He traveled with enough raw materials so that, when inspired, he could do a little design as well as repair work.

Continuing to share his thoughts, Jake rose, retrieved the *moka* pot, leaned in over Lily, and poured more steaming coffee into her glass. Just inches away from him, watching him intently talk and pour, her eyes moved over him, studying his body up close, that fascinating understated combination of strength and grace to his movements.

He pulled back and poured more coffee for himself, continuing to talk about science and the elements and old pyrotechnic traditions. Lily leaned back in her chair, cupping the coffee in her hands, taking in the night sounds of the field and the rich scent from her glass and the intensity of this man. It was mesmerizing to hear him speak about his work, thrilling to be near him while he did so, indeed, like listening to a poet speaking about words, an artist discussing paints, a man talking to a woman about love. Being so near such ardor gave Lily a heady feeling, as though some kind of intoxicant was flowing into her bloodstream.

He had no reason with which she was accustomed for doing the things he did with fireworks. This was not a man talking about business or college football or golfing. This was a man who had something to say that went far beyond any of that, that rose above the limits of spoken language. Lily realized that Jake Russo had no reason to pursue his craft the way he did other than the need to express himself, to stir, to touch. Listening to him talk, captivated, she again found her mind wandering and wondered what it would be like to be the focus of such a man capable of such desire. What would it be like to be wanted by him?

She continued looking at him, thinking about him this way, and realized how much these feelings were overcoming her. His gaze into her was so deep and so true— could she really keep these inner thoughts from him? Her heart began to panic. Could he hear it? Lily found herself overtaken with a nervousness, a lack of control she'd never really felt before. She couldn't seem to catch her breath.

What was she doing? Of course she was getting nervous. It was getting late. Much later than the time that two people who were simply sharing a meal were still together. *Is this what he is thinking, too?* she wondered. She could ask for more coffee. But she didn't really want more coffee. No, she needed to get home. Of course she needed to get home. She had a house to put together. A kitchen to organize. A husband who would soon be returning. A husband! Why then was she still sitting here? What was she waiting for? What was *he* waiting for?

"Well, I've got mortars to set at sunup."

There. It was time for her to go. She took a deep breath, feeling a discordant mixture of strong emotions, mainly relief and regret, strangely at odds with each other. "Yes. I have a lot to do tomorrow." She stood up.

He stood, too. And he just looked at her for a long moment, close to her; finally, that curious smile of his that was less of a smile and more of an expression of knowing beyond what was being spoken took hold of his lips.

"What?" asked Lily lightly, breathlessly.

"When I saw you in that field, your hair back, your face looking up into the sky, the breeze blowing your dress against you . . . I thought you were a ghost."

"A ghost?"

"A spirit that had come for me."

"I'm just a girl, Jake."

"I think you're that, and much, much more."

Another long moment. Lily found herself returning his smile, finding her own sense of knowing. And suddenly she felt at ease, a sense of mysterious calm.

"I should go," she said.

"Yes."

They exchanged the expected niceties about the dinner as Jake walked Lily through the field to her car. But there was a detectable bit of distance. A quietness. They did not talk much. They just strolled together in the lambent moonlight, the grass licking at their legs, a lovely ballad crooning slowly from the truck radio in the distance. The night had come to an end, and inauthentic pleasantries about staying in touch seemed more than forced and silly. To utter the speech of daily life was to diminish the simple but rare closeness and truth that they had shared on this night, a night that was already becoming memory.

They came to the Packard. As she reached for the handle of the door, Lily half expected another hand to appear from the darkness and grasp hers and pull her away from the car and keep her from leaving. But of course that did not happen. Lily opened the door to the Packard and got in.

Sitting behind the wheel, the door wide open, she looked up at him. He put his hand on the open door and leaned in toward her. She saw the muscles in his shoulders and arms expand and become clearly defined through his thin shirt as he did this, and again she found herself intrigued by his subtle strength.

The moonlight on their faces, they looked deeply into each other. And right then Lily felt that the simplicity and purity of this moment must surely have some purpose or plan beyond the plain serendipity of things coming together, and as she closed her eyes, in a lingering blink, her pulse racing, she was sure that right now at this second this moment was being repeated a thousand times across the planet in a thousand thousand heartbeats, all part of some great and natural design of connection driving human beings together through forces of attraction and affection.

He moved ever so slightly closer to her, lips seemingly parting, and Lily felt sure that he was about to kiss her. As she felt an instant surging in her blood and an electric current through her nerves at the realization that she might have to decide how to respond, she saw that he was not coming any closer.

She just stared at him, pondering. Had he changed his mind? Had she imagined it? Was she the one initiating it? She suddenly realized that she was sitting in this car, but she wasn't starting it. She was ready to stay and ready to go, the maddening battle between impulse and reason getting worse than whatever fate action had in store. While instincts deep inside pushed her to lean forward, toward him, she willed these forces to stop. It was time to go home.

"It was nice meeting you," she said. "Good luck in your travels."

Jake just continued looking at her. *What is he thinking?* she wondered. What was going through his head? Finally, smiling to her, he said, "Lily, *anche se il cielo già è riempito di stelle, potete fare sempre il vostri propri.*"

"One of your father's sayings?" she asked.

"Yes," he said. "Even though the sky is already filled with stars, you can always make your own."

As she took that in, Jake shut her door and stepped back from the car. She started the ignition. After a moment, she put the Packard in gear and drove off down Owl Swamp Road.

DREAMS

Slowly steering the Packard up her driveway, Lily parked it next to Paul's Cadillac
in the garage behind the house. She had
made a mental note earlier in the day to
get Paul's big car washed before he came
home, but she didn't want to think about
that right now and left the garage quickly.

Making her way up the rear walkway,
Lily entered the back door and turned on
the lights in the kitchen. The unpacked
boxes were still there, just as unpacked
as they were this morning. Lily sighed.
When she started her day, she never would
have guessed that this was how it would

have turned out. In the familiarity of the brightly lit white-tiled kitchen, the last few hours seemed dreamlike and surreal. However, like a schoolgirl who doesn't want to get up, Lily wanted the dream to last.

She kicked off her dirty sandals, walked out of the kitchen, and headed for the stairs. However, before she went up them, she walked right into a pile of hanging clothes she'd recently thrown from an unpacked box. She scooped up an armful and ascended the stairs, mindlessly dangling clothing behind her.

She entered her bedroom and turned on a single lamp. Its mica shade cast a flesh-toned glow throughout the room. Walking by her lovely four-poster bed, she slowed and looked at it for a moment. *How silly*, she thought, *the bedrooms in movies where even married people slept in separate beds*. Was the closeness shared in a single bed really so morally unacceptable that simply suggesting it on-screen was shameful?

Carrying the clothes, Lily went to her closet, moved aside a row of hanging dresses, and began to hang up the new additions. Straightening them, her fingers came across the pearled bodice of her wedding dress. She caressed the silk throughout the flowing full skirt and held a pearl bead in her hand. Wedding gowns were one of the only items exempt from the cloth restrictions imposed by the War Production Board, but most people used rayon, a new synthetic material made from wood pulp, saving silk for parachutes. However, Honey was not most people and she insisted on the silk, obtained from cocoons of the Chinese mulberry worms, the absolute finest of course, and the dress was simply stunning. So beautiful. So much effort for something that lasted such a short time, Lily thought. Then she smiled, remembering: *A moment in the sky, forever in the heart*. She let go of the bead and took in the silky dress, hanging hollow and lifeless, its inhabitant long gone.

Walking into the bathroom, Lily switched on the bright lights, a little taken aback by the thin trail of dirt she realized she had tracked in. Putting the stopper in the drain of the large clawfoot bathtub, she turned on the water, drawing a hot stream into the tub. Unbuttoning her dress, she let it fall to the floor. She took off her slip, unclasped her bra, and removed her underwear. Realizing that her hair was a mess, she shook it out, and errant pieces of dried grass fell to the tiled floor.

Being this dirty was most certainly something strange for Lily. She took in the sight of her soil-stained dress lying rumpled—how different from the gowns in her closet—and the feeling of her skin, matte with dirt and dried perspiration, and she smiled, enjoying the carefree sensations running through her. Forgotten memories came over her, of when she was ten, returning home from a camping trip, and when she was twelve, playing in the creek with her friends, even when she was seventeen, planting corn out in the gardens at Holly Hills, something her mother hated because it wasn't appropriate for a woman of marrying age to work in the dirt.

Feeling as she did now reminded her how much had changed since then, before she was married, when doing these kinds of things seemed so natural.

Running her hands down her body, she thought, too, about how much she had physically changed over the last few years. She'd lost much of the adolescent plumpness, the "baby fat," her mother called it, that she had three years ago. Her breasts were rounded and firm, her stomach flat, her hips curved but slender. Her figure was much more defined and shapely, more womanly. What would Paul think of her now? she wondered. Would he like her like this? Would he even recognize her?

Lily squinted a little as specks of sharp light, refracted from her engagement ring, shot across her face as she removed it and put it aside on the counter. People often noticed the heavy ring, which seemed its point, but how strange the metal and polished gemstone looked on the counter, alone and cold. What was it like, she wondered, when the diamond was pulled from the ground, covered in dirt and soil, unadulterated and pure? She removed the ring from the counter and placed it in a drawer.

Lily turned off the bright lights, allowing only the soft glow from the mica-shaded lamp to illuminate the bathroom. That was better. Then she slipped into the bath and, when the water level was near the top, turned off the faucet handles with her foot. Leaning back, eyes closed, Lily felt herself lulled by the warmth. After letting the water soothe her for a moment, she picked up a bar of soap and a razor and began to shave her legs, as she did almost every day. Her girlfriends balked when they found out that Lily did this. Why shave so much if your husband is away? But Lily liked the way it made her feel, something she did for herself, a purely womanly action that was part of her daily routine.

Three years of living alone and she would soon have a man in her house. Three years of sleeping alone and she would soon have a man in her bed. She relished the idea of Paul coming home, but she was increasingly aware these past few weeks that it was the *idea* of Paul more than the reality of him that she relished. Paul was like the lead in an old movie short, a loop that ran over and over in the cinema of her head. While there were a handful of quick, barely comprehensible phone conversations and a series of congenial letters, the movie was set in the past. A tall blond young man in a seersucker suit impassively watching her eat an ice-cream sundae on a hot summer night. On a picnic in the forest, she talks excitedly about the beauty all around them, and he just watches her, not sharing her interest in the plants and the birds, not even understanding it, just watching, and finally silencing her with a kiss. Two virgins splayed and ungainly as newborn birds rolling around on brand-new sheets in a brand-new bed.

Her smooth legs, the warm water lifting and cradling her body; a bath always made her feel good, but tonight even more so than usual. Her eyes naturally shut as her mind quieted and thoughts slipped in and out—images and dreams and feelings. But it wasn't Paul's face that she saw. It was Jake, in the moonlit field, blowing on her knee, running his hands on her legs, his dark eyes on her.

The thoughts and sensations were strong and fierce, but instead of rushing them, Lily let them linger. Though she felt guilty at her mental betrayal, she didn't want to extinguish the vision of Jake just yet. She wanted to savor and reexamine the moment.

Lily put her hands on the edges of the tub, sinking a little deeper in the water, and thought about the man in the field. The way his body felt on top of her when he leapt to her protection—pushing into her back as the burning embers fell around them. His scent. His breath in her ear.

Quickly she stood up, breaking the dreamlike trance and letting the water drip off her body, and stepped out of the bath. She grabbed a thick towel and slowly dried herself off, then pulled the plug, letting the water drain, taking the memories of Jake with it.

Taking another towel from a nearby stack, Lily began to dry her hair. She sat in front of the mirror, too lost in thought and emotion to really pay much attention to her reflection, and meditatively brushed out her hair for a long time. When it was generally dry, she brushed her teeth and applied some cocoa butter, from a block given to her by her father, to her face. As she began to walk out of the bathroom, smelling clean, feeling warm and relaxed, she came across her dress and underwear lying on the floor, dirt on them and around them. Lily picked up the clothes and the scent of them immediately transported her back to the field, and dinner, and Jake Russo— images and feelings that simply did not want to leave.

Lily tossed the clothes in a hamper,

walked out of the bathroom, turned off the lamp, and got into bed. So much on her mind, but she felt warm and cradled and comfortable.

From her bed she could see pictures on her dresser and nightstand—one of herself and Paul sitting together at Holly Hills, another of Paul in his uniform, smiling at her. Looking at those beautifully framed photographs was part of her evening routine and it always grounded her before sleep, but tonight she did not feel such footing and her mind drifted, mulling over the images and sensations from the day.

She looked at the stars from her bedroom window. So many of them, in the same place they always were; how could you see a blank slate?

Finally, with the stars and Jake and the pictures of Paul floating in the restless pools of her mind, she fell asleep.

July 1, 1945, just before dawn

A little before sunrise, Lily opened her eyes feeling surprisingly full of energy. As she lay there, cozy soft sheets all around her body, head deep in pillows and hair tossed out among them, Jake Russo was immediately on her mind, the way he had listened to her, the way he seemed to understand her. No, he *did* understand her. But she wanted to understand *him* more, she wanted to unravel the puzzle that was this mysterious stranger in the field.

She loved this time of morning when the world was waking but dreams were still palpable. But soon it would be day, and Lily had quite a lot to do, and here she was still lying around thinking about him. Somehow, she had to get this man and yesterday out of her mind and come back to the present and come back to reality. She took a deep breath and rose. She put on an oversized shirt and headed downstairs.

The cool oak-planked floors on her bare feet, Lily made her way into the kitchen, scooted around the boxes, opened the refrigerator, and got a Coke. Finally finding an opener, she popped off the cap, tossed it across the room into the garbage, and took a deep drink. Looking around the kitchen, Lily felt her insides sink at the mess and the realness of it all. She so much preferred the wonderful thoughts and feelings of upstairs, and she felt guilty about that, but guilt did little to assuage this truth.

She took another swig of her Coke—oh, how she loved the carbonation sliding down her throat, the caffeinated coldness hitting and expanding in her stomach, waking the rest of her body moments later.

On the balls of her feet, a childhood habit, Coke in hand, Lily made her way across the foyer, opened the front door, and walked outside.

She inhaled deeply, tossing her head back, the air a fresh blanket, warm and pine scented. A sparrowlark cooed from a mist-covered fence post. Lily sat down in one of the high-backed rocking chairs and sipped her morning Coke. The midsummer sun rose behind the house, but the western sky, which the porch oversaw, was still dark with dawdling night. She sat and rocked and awaited the dawn.

This was her home, and in just a few days her husband was going to walk up these steps and slip his hands around her body and kiss her, just as he had three years ago when he left, and she would begin her life. But there was something about the way she felt—perhaps it was the lingering images of Jake, the sensations of his cooking, the sentiments that he had brought out in her over dinner, his touch on her leg, her thoughts about him in the bath, his passion—and as much as she tried, or didn't try but knew she should, she just couldn't seem to shake it, and him, from her mind. And now all these things seemed even more evocative and alive at this magic moment, this middle moment, in the diffuse gray between night and day, between emotion and reason, that made her feel that she was on some kind of a precipice, like she had some kind of decision to make and with each passing second the sun continued its rise and the sky changed its tones and a pressing sensation gripped her breathing tighter and tighter like something was about to break and in moments rush out and be forever gone. She took another gulp of the sweet caramel drink and looked out.

Without warning of any kind, a silver needle shot into the sky, perforating the great expanse of dark fabric before her and trailing a thread of flittering brilliant white sparks. Then there was a dull boom and a spherical explosion of red stars, followed by another burst, twice as big, of green stars and, five seconds later, a massive, nearly unfathomable, torrent of yellow. And a quick flash, and the stars began to fade and fall.

It was the firework Jake had described to Lily last night. And seeing it before her like this, moving from mind to sky, from memory to actuality, from dreams to reality, made it seem as though the whole of nature had conjured its forces, animal and elemental alike, to move her. It was more than a sign. It was more than an appeal to her heart. In a world of rules, of men in uniforms, of clearly defined right and wrong and good and evil, it was an urgent and critical plea to listen to instinct, to take a chance.

MISSED CALLS

Lily pulled the Packard over to the side of Owl Swamp Road, turned off the engine, and hopped out, shutting the door behind her. Still low over the flatland east, the sun threw long aureate light across the field. Lily walked out into it, the high grass around her arched and wet and swaying in the breeze.

Jake was already hard at work, digging long trenches to bury mortars, when Lily approached. For a moment, she had a flash of what Jake must have looked like in the battlefields of Europe.

He stopped, rested an arm on the shovel,

and took in the sight of her coming toward him. Freshly scrubbed face, hair neatly pulled back, walking into the sun in a pretty, tailored summer dress, Lily was a stunning vision. An angel gilded in the haze. Jake felt his pulse quicken involuntarily as he just stared, fixedly, at her.

"I saw your firework this morning," Lily said.

"I wasn't ready to sleep last night after you left. So I worked on it."

"It was incredible."

He continued to stare. Once again, she let him. He'd certainly been attracted to women before, but he couldn't remember ever feeling this unsteady. As beautiful as she had been over the candlelight during dinner, as lovely as she had been in his memory of her throughout the night, to see her like this, fresh and clean and radiant in the silken daylight, she literally took his breath away. *Get a grip, buddy*, he told himself. He willed himself to inhale deeply, slowing his heart rate. He wiped the sweat from his brow. "Would you like some breakfast?" he said slowly, controlling the cadence of his words. "I've already had mine, but I could find something for you."

"No, thank you. I can't stay long. And actually, I was thinking perhaps I could offer you a meal."

"No pie?" he said with a disarming grin.

"I'll leave the pecan pies to the Auxiliary," she said, returning the smile. "I was thinking, maybe, lunch. Are you free for it today?"

"Maybe a late lunch. I have to get these twenty-fours in the ground." He pointed to a stack of big two-foot-across steel mortars.

"How about two-ish?"

"Sure. But it gets pretty hot out here 'bout then."

"I know a place nearby where it's cooler. I think you'd really like it. We can eat there."

"Sounds great."

"Good. See you this afternoon."

Lily headed back to her car. Jake watched her for a long moment, and then he returned to his labor, digging with increased tempo.

A shopping basket in hand, Lily made her way through the aisles at the market. She found some corn, picked it up, and smelled it. The husks were slightly browned from the heat, and while the corn was fine, Lily knew it would taste nothing like the fresh summer corn she loved so much that grew out at Holly Hills. That was what she somehow got stuck in her mind today, that sweet Georgia Indian corn, and simply nothing else would do today. She put the browned corn back and continued her shopping, realizing that Mrs. Keener was observing her.

"Good morning, Lily."

"Good morning, Mrs. Keener."

"You look pretty today."

"Thank you."

"Did you see the fireworks this morning?"

"Yes. I did." Lily put a loaf of fresh wheat bread in her basket.

"Have you ever seen anything so beautiful?"

"No, ma'am, I don't believe I have."

"Evelyn Tabor hired the pyrotechnics man for the Auxiliary. Says he's a quiet fellow. Keeps to himself."

"Huh."

"Italian."

Lily raised her eyebrows as best she could.

"Mrs. Brown said she saw him camping

out there in Bartam's Field, not far from your parents'."

"Do you have any roasting chicken to-day?"

Mrs. Keener removed a just-plucked chicken from a refrigerator behind the counter and wrapped it in brown wax paper. "Are you and Paul going to watch the show from Holly Hills on the Fourth?"

"Haven't decided yet, Mrs. Keener."

"What am I saying? You probably won't leave your house for a week when that boy comes home." Mrs. Keener winked at Lily as she handed her the chicken. Lily produced a smile.

While Mrs. Keener rang up her items, Lily looked out the big glass windows at the front of the store. There was great excitement on the streets of Toccoa right now. Men in uniform poured into town and it seemed as though the entire world was celebrating.

Looking over her shoulder, down an aisle stacked high with cornflake boxes, Lily saw a young man in a Navy uniform and a young woman, her hair a mess, holding each other and kissing. The woman playfully tried to break away, swatting at him and trying to tuck her hair in place, but the sailor held her tight and kept kissing her. They laughed, looking around to make sure no one was watching, unable to keep their hands off each other.

Without them noticing, Lily continued looking, smiling whimsically to herself, surprised by the mixture of joy and restlessness she felt.

After a short drive just north of town, Lily pulled off 123 and onto the paved driveway of Holly Hills. She told herself she was going there to get the rest of her clothes as her mother had told her to do, but mainly she was thinking about that corn.

Mixed among the pines and hardwoods of her family's fifty-five-acre estate were scores of fully mature southern magnolias. They lined the drive leading up the hill to the house. During the early summer, the massive hundred-foot trees were covered with huge white flowers that filled all of Holly Hills with the ethereal scent of citronella. By July, though, the flowers and leaves burned and curled in the heat. And by August, vast piles of brown droppings lay dead and decomposing under and all around the trees.

When Lily was in grammar school, a UGA English professor who bought a house in town wrote an article that was published in *The Toccoa Record* calling the southern magnolias "Toccoa's sacred cows." Likening the town's grand trees to the bovines that wandered the streets of Hindu countries rubbed many people the wrong way, though it was the professor's practice of yoga in public parks that ultimately got her run out of town.

Lily parked her car in front of the stately house, a white-columned antebellum structure that "crowned the hills," as people liked to say. She stepped out of the car and took in the big, heady fragrance of the magnolias. She closed her eyes, committing the scent to memory, knowing the late summer burn-off and drop were coming very soon.

To the side of the house, a massive mound of Cherokee roses grew over and around the old caretaker's cabin, now a toolshed. Lily loved the wild roses and insisted they be left to their own designs.

Honey reluctantly acquiesced and steered the gardeners clear. Lily had even wanted to use the rambling white roses at her wedding, but they weren't in bloom yet, to her mother's relief. Hothouse orchids, exotic but decidedly controlled, were flown in.

Lily entered the house, walking through the spacious foyer. There was a scent to her childhood home, coffee and vanilla and her father's sweet pipe tobacco, but it was more than that, and she couldn't quite articulate it, but it was distinct and strong and always triggered unexpected flashes of moments from her life. Riding a tricycle her father gave her all around the foyer on some wonderful early birthday. Thousands of jasmine gardenias decorating the entire downstairs for her friend Jenna's trousseau party. Lily's brother, in his officer's uniform, walking out the door for the last time. The Army chaplain coming through that same door with the news.

After, Honey never spoke of Lily's brother, at least not openly. It was Honey's way and it was not questioned, and Lily understood that this was not a subject to be brought up, so she didn't. There were very few pictures or items of his around the house, but

Honey did keep one framed photo of him on a lovely jade-topped table against the staircase in the foyer. Lily loved that picture. He was so handsome and hopeful and determined. Looking at the picture sometimes she would recall the way he would smile at her and call her "kiddo." As a girl, she remembered always liking that. "Hiya, kiddo," he would say, and then run off with his older friends.

Lily walked up the big staircase, down the upstairs hallway, and into the bedroom that was hers from birth.

She turned on the light, went to the closet, and removed the remaining clothing that still hung there. Most everything she felt she wanted close had already been moved to her new home. This was the last of it. She slung the clothes over her arm and took a final look around to see if she'd missed anything: ribbons from horseback riding, a handmade birthday card her friend Jenna had given her, a silly old necklace Lily had made from tiny glass beads one summer. These things were all important to her. But they were from a different time, a different place, different from where she was and where she was going.

In a stack of schoolbooks lying on a desk, a large yearbook from Toccoa High caught Lily's eye. She picked it up, smiling as she thumbed through it. Tucked away in the pages was a lovely charcoal drawing on paper torn from a sketch pad: a girl with wet hair in a slip, leaning back on her arms, face to the sky, eyes closed. Lily smiled as the drawing brought a new flash of memory to her mind, of that day four years ago, so long ago now, when she went swimming with Mark Morgan and he drew her in the sun. Everyone always said he was so wild, the lanky carefree boy whose father worked in the back of the Feed & Seed store, but Lily remembered thinking that Mark was also sweet and smart and filled with dreams of such interesting things that were just too fanciful and strange for the tastes of most folks in town. After she met Paul, Lily never thought much about Mark Morgan, never saw him again, except in the reception line at his wedding, when he married Jenna. Odd, even funny, the paths life offers, and the path one chooses.

Lily secured the drawing back in the yearbook and closed it, and fighting a swirl

of emotions, she looked around her childhood room one more time, taking in her
frilly childhood bed where she so many
times dreamed about the shape and sub-
stance of the days she was now living. The
feelings wept into her heart like a pad of
butter on warm grits.

Then she turned off the light and, carrying her clothes, walked out of her room.

After dumping the clothes in the back of
the Packard, Lily walked from the car
around to the side of the house, past the
old shed overgrown with the Cherokee
roses—evidence that a gardener once
lived there, she always thought—continuing
past a low rusted iron fence that surrounded
a small gathering of mossy tombstones,
Civil War era mostly, until she reached a
large vegetable plot that had been cut into
a far corner of the back lawn. This was the
Davis family's garden. GiGi, who worked
for the family and lived in a room inside the
main house, often hired local boys to help
tend the garden, which provided a variety
of fresh herbs and vegetables for the family. Despite her efforts, the garden was not

in the best of shape, having been regularly picked over by the deer.

As a girl, Lily loved working out here, and sometimes her father would join her if he was in town. Using their bare hands they would spread compost in the fall, sow tomatoes and okra and green peppers in the spring, and sit out in the dirt and picnic with their fresh vegetables in the summer. Honey enjoyed seeing them together, but as Lily grew older, Honey grew less tolerant of her daughter's gardening. Even calling the plot a Victory Garden did little to assuage Honey's belief that the dirt was no place for a young lady.

Taking in the wonderful smell of the warm earth, Lily went straight to the rows of Indian corn, an extra-sweet variety that flourished throughout the area until the Cherokee were removed from the land, forced west by settlers.

Lily pulled the green stalks down with her hands, shaking off the dirt and plucking off ears of corn. The smell of the husks and corn silk brought a rush of memories to mind and it seemed like only a few days ago that she and her father would sit out here and talk about the silliest things, which would always make her laugh. She smiled, remembering. He used to say that he wanted to take a pot of boiling water out here and drop the corn right in it, that's how fresh he liked it, and they'd laugh till they were rolling in the dirt thinking about what Honey would say and do if she found them out here with one of her good pots boiling up produce.

Lily brought the freshly picked corn to her face and felt the husks on her skin and breathed in its sweetness, and a sigh escaped from her.

Back at her home, listening to the radio, lost in thought, Lily sat on the back porch shucking corn under heavens flaxy and creamed as raw butter from cows on summer pasture. She loved doing this, especially on these kinds of warm afternoons. It was as close to cooking as Lily got.

When she finished removing all the husks from the Indian corn, Lily cut the kernels off the cob with a chef's knife, letting them drop into a large casserole pot. Using the back of the knife, she scraped the milk from the cobs, which she also let drip off into the pot.

Taking the pot into the house, Lily added some sugar, salt, flour, and butter and put it in the preheated oven. She smiled, quite satisfied with her improvised work, which was not entirely unlike a brownie dish she had learned from Honey years ago. But rather than follow a recipe, Lily trusted her instinct. *After all*, she thought, *with sugar and butter and corn this good, how can you go wrong?*

She checked on the chicken that was boiling on top of the stove in an oversized hammered-copper stockpot that she'd dug out of a Rich's gift box, a lavish house-warming present from one of her father's business associates whose name she could not recall. She remembered several lengthy conversations with the mid-level manager who seemed to feel that paying attention to Mr. Davis's child at holiday parties would be beneficial to his career. The booty of a childhood spent smiling through such proceedings surrounded her now. Silver tongs from Tiffany's. Fine china from Wedgwood. Everyday dishware from Davison's. Cutlery from J. B. White. Utensils from Kirven's. All manner of bowls and bakeware from Belk-Gallant downtown.

There were also a few pieces of heirloom crystal and silver, harbingers of the riches her mother had in store for her. Lily felt a twinge of guilt presently using these items, many that came with cards referencing meals to be made for Paul, but she put this out of her mind.

She added some bay leaves and fresh garden carrots to the stock and it smelled wonderful. Lily knew that her mother would take great issue with her boiling a good roaster this way. She had listened to Honey's recipes for fowl ad nauseam, but this was the one fail-safe way Lily knew. And at the end of the day, even if it was prosaic and "common," this was in fact the way that Lily preferred her chicken.

The black plastic handle on the white Lux minute timer, a gift from the Chattanooga cousins, clicked to the zero and the tinny bell instantly began to ring.

Lily removed the chicken from the pot and the casserole dish from the oven. When they were cool, she wrapped slices of chicken and corn soufflé casserole in wax paper and put them into one of the Keener's heavy paper sacks. She dropped in the fresh bread. Then she removed several Cokes from the coldest part of the refrigerator and put them in the sack to keep everything cool.

Looking at the clock, Lily grabbed the sack, turned off the radio, and bolted out the kitchen door. She'd put much more effort into the cooking than she had planned and she was running late.

As she headed for the Packard parked in the side driveway, the telephone began to ring inside the house, but already in the car with the ignition started, Lily did not hear it. She drove off, and the phone continued to ring and ring.

By the creek on the edge of the field, shirt removed, Jake splashed cool water on his face and cleaned up. From where he was standing, he could see the tops of several hundred mortar pipes protruding from the ground in neat lines. They looked like the helmets of infantrymen, dug into trenches, prepared for battle. Jake stuck his head right into the rippling brook and shook off the image of war, the shock of the cool water soothing and therapeutic.

During the morning he'd made very good progress, and the break was a welcome relief. His muscles were sore, but he undeniably liked this feeling—his body telling him that he'd done a good day's work. During his time overseas he developed a keen appreciation for his body and an understanding of its workings. It had taken him up impossibly steep hills during long, hard fights where exhaustion meant death. Of all the pounds of equipment he carried in war, his own machine was the one that saved him time and time again. Skin taut across flesh, musculature visibly outlined, he moved fluidly, sinuously, his body honed from both calculated labor and the natural instincts born of survival. Grace belying strength.

Drying his chest with a small towel, Jake recognized that he had lost some weight. He made a mental note to try to eat more, as his mother was always pleading with him to do. He loved his mother so and he smiled, thinking about her.

They kicked the door open at 1:27 in the morning. The splintering wood of the door frame was loud, but his mother's screams were louder. She spoke no English and the uniformed men spoke no Italian. They

wore brown suits, brown ties, brown over-
coats. Soggy fedoras. Side holsters with
.45-caliber automatics. They flashed their
badges in cursory fashion and attempted
to locate and identify the man for whom
they had come as quickly and profession-
ally as possible. But of course the screaming made this difficult on all counts.

"Ernesto Russo? Ernesto Russo?"

The men read from a document dripping with freezing rain. RESIDENT ALIEN was
printed in big red block lettering.

The men grabbed him as he walked
into the foyer, unshaven, dazed, tying his
bathrobe. More screaming. Pleading in
Italian. She grabbed a picture frame off
the wall. Thrusting it at them. A letter of
thanks signed by Herbert Hoover. But they
pushed her aside and they took him away
as fast as they could, his slippers filling
with sleet as they marched him to the
brown car and shoved him into the back.

Jake plunged his head in the creek again,
shutting down memories once more. He
yanked it out and shook his head, sending
water flying from his hair. Then he removed
a small black comb from a pocket in his

jeans and pulled it through his wet hair. He put on a clean shirt and began to walk back into the field.

As Jake approached his truck, he saw Lily walking toward him, the sun behind her, looking even more fresh and beautiful than she had that morning.

Lily waved at him.

He waved back.

The sun climbed over the top of Lily's house and began its descent into the western horizon. The high-backed rockers, swaying ever so slightly in the afternoon Currahee breeze, cast the beginnings of their shadows along the front porch.

Inside the empty house, the phone rang.

COMING HOME

The tall, broad-shouldered man stood in the open aircraft hangar and held a telephone receiver to his ear.

"Come on, pick up."

Frustrated that no one was answering, he ran a hand through his fine blond hair.

The cord of the heavy phone ran back into a communications office where two British officers administered the overseas calls. Through the heavy glass window of the office, they watched the man attentively. Indeed, they had been given clear orders to take good care of him.

But the man did not look happy. He

glanced repeatedly outside the hangar where a Douglas C-54 transport plane gunned its four engines, ready for a quick takeoff.

Night was falling and the fog rolled in off the Channel. Soon all of South Britain would be socked in. If the C-54 didn't get off the ground immediately, air traffic control would most certainly delay the flight until tomorrow, no matter how much weight this man's company could throw around.

"Where are you, Lils?" he said into the phone.

One of the British officers took an incoming call in the communications office. The officer nodded repeatedly, put down the phone, and stepped out, approaching the man.

"Sir, the tower says you have to go now."

"Five more minutes."

"Sir, the other passengers are waiting."

Another man, wearing the U.S. Army uniform of a lieutenant colonel, jogged into the hangar.

"Paul, the pilot says if we don't leave right now we'll miss our flight window. If you want to get home early we have to go.

Come on, you can call her when we land in Macon."

The fair-haired man, slender and a bit drawn, as though he'd aged more than he should have over the last few years, nodded to his friend and handed the receiver to one of the British officers, who terminated the call.

"You know what, maybe I'll just show up on the front doorstep and surprise her."

"Excellent idea, pal," the lieutenant colonel said, clapping Paul on the back. "Women love surprises."

The men ran for the plane.

KUDZU AND BROKEN GLASS

This is absolutely incredible," said Jake. "I think this may be the most beautiful place I've ever been."

Lily and Jake walked through the dense, lush forest, wayfarers stumbling into some paradise. They followed an overgrown path through the woodland, shaded and fecund and undisturbed. Luxuriant ferns, leaves fat and thick, grew waist high. A rich carpet of pine needles covered the earth underfoot. Just ahead lay the burbling bend of a creek, its rocks soft with lichen and moss.

"Everything on the other side of the creek

all the way down to Highway One-twenty-three is part of Holly Hills," said Lily.

"So basically your family owns a small country."

"See that clearing way out there? Next to Bartam's Field? After the War Between the States, my grandfather had those meadows planted with long staple Creole cotton. Acres and acres of it. The best mills all over the South bought from Holly Hills."

"What happened?"

"Sea Island."

"That's good cotton."

"And cheaper." Jake carried the sack Lily had packed as they continued on into the woods. The farther in they went, the denser it became. "My father went to law school, the land went untended, and my parents dug a swimming pool and contented themselves with barbeques in the backyard. But I, on the other hand, came out here quite a lot."

A big grin grew on Lily's face and Jake could see the mischief in her. He liked it.

They talked playfully, effortlessly, the conversation bouncing in a seamless montage of childhood anecdotes and favorite foods and hopes and dreams and wishes.

Lily said that she always loved coming out here because the woods transported her to the magical far-off places she'd read about in Thoreau and John Muir. Her favorite was to imagine she was in the spellbound forest from *A Midsummer Night's Dream*. "I'm a great dreamer and armchair traveler," Lily confessed. "In truth, I've actually only been out of Georgia once."

"To where?"

"Chattanooga. I visited the Ruby Falls caves when I was ten. They were amazing, filled with these huge stalactites and flowstone formations, millions of years old. It's nature's art. But my dream, as silly and trite as it sounds, is to visit Paris someday. I want to see the art in the Louvre more than anything."

"The greatest art I saw in Paris wasn't in the Louvre," Jake replied. "It was on the sidewalk outside. Literally right on the sidewalk. In chalk. I don't know the woman's name, but I watched her work all day and into much of the night. Patrons came and went from the cafés, watching her sketch, but she didn't even notice. She just concentrated wholly and entirely on her work. She drew a complex portrait of a ship at sea, completely from memory. The details were perfect. It was magnificent."

Once again, Lily could hear that unique passion in Jake Russo's voice, see it in his eyes.

"It rained late that night in Paris," he continued, and then paused, remembering. "My dream is to create something equally inspired someday."

When they got to the creek, Jake took Lily's hands and helped her across the slick rocks. In truth, this was an easy task for her—because of her frequent trips here she could nearly navigate the rocks blindfolded—but she took his hand nonetheless. And at once, his touch sent sudden and unexpected warmth through her. How could something as simple and sweet as holding hands be so erotic? Even remembering the moment on the truck, with his hand on her knee, sent a new rush, involuntary and feverish, through her body.

The creek's spattering flow dampened their clothing. Lily felt her dress, a light cornflower blue floral print, clinging to her body. This was the sort of thing that was supposed to make a proper Toccoa girl wary and self-conscious, but Lily didn't care.

After crossing the creek, Jake let her hand go, but the sensation of his touch remained like a spell. What was happening? Yesterday morning her life was perfect. She knew exactly what she wanted, husband and house on the hill. And she had it. She had it all. But that had changed. In a flash, in a few clicks of the minute timer, all her desires had changed and she wanted something else. But how could she be with this beautiful, passionate dark-haired man and keep the rest of the world intact? She couldn't, and she knew that. The world beyond these magical woods, the real world, had rules, and she had signed up for them.

Lily took in a deep breath of the fragrant forest air, sighing as she released it—she loved these woods so.

"Do you hear that?" Jake said, stopping for a moment. "That rushing sound."

The playful grin again came over Lily's face and she stopped, too. "It's the legend."

"What legend?"

"The legend of Toccoa." She stood very close to him as he listened. "The Cherokee lived all through this area before the settlers came. Stephens County was the heart of their nation. As the story goes, Toccoa was an Indian princess, the most beautiful in the tribe—'Toccoa' is the Cherokee word for 'beautiful.' One summer afternoon, she was out alone in the forest and she met a young warrior from an enemy tribe named Wild Waters with long black hair, deep dark eyes, who spoke as sweetly as the scent of Cherokee roses. Naturally, they fell in love."

"Naturally," said Jake, enjoying this.

"But Toccoa's father had already betrothed her to a man in their tribe and he refused to let her see Wild Waters of the enemy nation."

"Why do fathers always do this sort of thing in old legends?"

"Good question. Mothers make much better antagonists."

Jake laughed. "So how does the story end?"

"Not well for Toccoa. There's a secret meeting planned between her and Wild Waters at the top of the falls, but there's some unseen moss and a very slippery boulder, and he jumps over after her, and, well—"

"Sounds like a cautionary tale."

"Oh yes, the ministers around here love telling it, but I think the ending is sweet."

"Which is?"

"That if you listen closely, with all your heart, you can hear Toccoa and her love's laughter in the creek."

Jake smiled at her, then tilted his head a little, listening. "I think I hear it."

"Yes. Me, too. I always think I can when I come out here. Of course, Toccoa Falls are just about a mile up the creek and some would say that's really what we're hearing."

"No, that's laughter. Definitely laughter."

"Early settlers reported seeing an Indian princess in the forest. The Cherokee said it was Toccoa, who had become one of the Nunnehi, one of the invisible people."

"The Nunnehi?" Jake said, asking for more.

"A spirit." Lily paused, a bit more serious now. Jake could tell that this was in fact something that was important to her, probably something she'd had in her head since she was a child. "Sometimes I think I see her, too."

Jake nodded, understanding. Then he looked around, taking in the beauty of this place. Lily just watched him, enjoying the sight of Jake, who seemed to have re-laxed since coming out here. He seemed brighter, airier. She watched as he closed his eyes, moved his head back, and took in the sounds and smells of the forest. Lily loved being able to take him here, give him this, and she wondered if this was how he felt about seeing her enjoy his cooking.

It was a lovely spot for a picnic, Lily thought. They could sit right there by the creek. But watching Jake take in the splen-dor and truly appreciate it in a way that no one else in her life, even Paul, ever had or really ever could prompted her to make a decision.

"Come on," she said to Jake, motioning. "I want to show you something."

Continuing their conversation, a con-stantly flowing stream of easy, fun, and sometimes intimate talk, the kind shared by close friends, they walked on, the growth thicker and shadier, flowering quince and mountain laurel forming rivulets of color all around them. Every few minutes they would slow to savor the natural enchantment of the wood.

If only there were some magic that would

allow her to turn back time, Lily secretly thought, to have met Jake before her marriage to Paul, before the war. Maybe on some level, that was why she took him here, to this place, where there were no signs of modern life, no cues from the real world. This path that she now walked was just as it was a hundred years ago. Just as it was throughout her childhood. It had always felt to her like a walk into the past. And now, more than ever, it seemed like a walk into a time when no fork in life's path had yet been encountered.

Suddenly she took his arm and stopped him. "There."

"What?"

"Do you see it?"

"I see kudzu. Lots and lots of kudzu."

"Look closer. It's right in front of you." She was enjoying this.

Jake stood in the small clearing and looked around. Kudzu was everywhere. During the early 1930s, the U.S. Soil Conservation Service had strongly encouraged southern farmers to plant the Asian vine in order to reduce erosion, a real problem with Georgia's infamous red clayous soil. But a bigger problem turned out to be that kudzu encountered no hard freeze in the South to keep it in check the way it did in its native Japan, so the plant quickly grew out of control. It crawled down from the rise above them, heading for the sustenance of the creek and engulfing everything in its path. The deciduous vine snaked up the great timeless pines. Like thick netting it covered whole coppices of young hardwoods. Thickets of sweet gum and wild dogwood were swathed entirely in its ponderous green leaves.

Finally, Lily leaned into him a little and pointed him to a huge mass of the vine, twenty feet high, thirty feet across, just down the path, directly in front of them. "Look, right there, right behind the clearing."

As he rose out of the top of the kudzu mass, Jake saw something that was decidedly man-made. "Is that a chimney?"

"Look closer."

"Whoa. It's a house."

"You might be a little generous with that term, but yes."

Jake walked right down to the kudzu-covered structure, as fascinated about this as Lily was about the firework she saw in the field. On closer examination, under the climbing broad-leaved vines Jake saw the shape of a shack, numerous panes of numerous windows, and the frame of a door. As he looked closer, he could see that the vines had been torn away from the windows and door, not in the last few days, but clearly someone had loosely tended to this place over the years.

"It was a sharecropper's cabin," Lily explained. "Come on."

Next to the overgrown path leading to the front of the door, Lily picked up a three-foot length of stick. It was worn and smooth, a tool created years ago. Jake watched, intrigued, as she used it to swipe some new kudzu shoots away from the front windows. Then she used the stick to clear and lift away shoots that had grown over the front door. She slowly turned the doorknob. Thick flakes of rust fell off. She eased the door open, snapping some rogue shoots that had succeeded in slipping through the door frame and were trying to explore the inside of the cabin.

Jake set the sack down and joined her, and watched with attentive amusement how excited she was to be here, and how entirely unfazed she was by the fresh spiderwebs on the doorjamb, which she brushed aside as she went inside.

The inside of the cabin was cool and clean. Startlingly so. But several of the windows were missing glass panes, and these openings, along with large gaps in the cabin's wood planking, created good ventilation. The kudzu mesh provided a natural screen. Jake had expected staleness and dust in the cabin, but instead it smelled of soft plants and living things. A few luna moth cocoons, vibrant and green, hung from a beam. To stand in the middle of the space was to feel the essence of the forest, a concentrate of its vigor and timelessness, as though the kudzu provided some sort of cover from temporal ravages.

Lily poked the stick through some of the open panes and used it to clear the lingering kudzu away from the windows, allowing even more light, gauzy columns of it, into the cabin. It was dream light, hued amber and celadon.

Jake looked around. The inside of the cabin was a single rectangular room, about three hundred square feet. Planks of wood covered most of the floor, though some areas of the red hard-packed dirt below lay exposed. One wall was anchored by a large river-stone fireplace. Another wall was lined with brick shelving. There was a small alcove with a few more shelves that looked like it might have been a pantry at one time. In a corner, there were some old camping supplies, a couple of Dietz kerosene barn lanterns, blankets, tarpaulins.

Jake examined a large shallow iron pan. "This is mining gear."

"The Georgia Gold Belt ran all along here, just north of the forest all the way to the Alabama border, not a good thing for the Cherokee, who were all forced to relocate west when it was discovered."

Lily produced an old tattered sheet of folded browned paper from one of the shelves and handed it to Jake. "Look," she said to him.

He opened it with great care. "It's an old map," he said with interest.

"Yes, of gold veins running under Auraria, a small town just a couple counties over."

Jake looked off for a moment, reflecting on the map and its meaning. "I wonder what happened to the people who lived here."

"Me, too. I've thought about it often."

"Think they got gold fever and went to Auraria?"

"My father and I stopped there once."

"What's it like?"

"Ghost town."

They both considered that for a moment, the image of a barren town washing over them.

"Wonder if they got there before all the gold was gone," Jake mused.

"I don't know, but there's something about walking down the empty streets of Auraria, wind knocking rotted shutters on the broken saloon, iron jail bars standing rusted in a heap of charred lumber . . . I always felt they should have stayed here in the woods."

Jake smiled at Lily as she stood in the middle of the cabin, seeing that she felt safe in this place.

Carefully refolding the map, he put it back and examined the shelving. Along with a few curious items, including a small collection of old ruined-looking oil paints, a small canister of wood glue, and a fairly clean Raggedy Ann doll, smile plastered on its face, there were a couple dozen Civil War–era bullets, presumably found nearby. Jake guessed them to be .44 and .50 calibers. Next to them were several tarnished brass buttons from an officer's uniform. Jake examined one, running his finger over the raised words SOUTH CARO- LINA, which surrounded a little palmetto, the state tree.

Lily retrieved the sack, removed the Cokes, and placed them under a loose floorboard near the wall where some dirt had been removed. The cold Georgia red clay served as a makeshift cooler. In the clay hole, next to the soft drinks, also pro- tected from the heat, was a Hoosier-style glass jar that contained a few clean tubes of oil paint.

Under the shelves Jake saw numerous Coca-Cola bottles, which were standing in a fairly large pile of broken bottle glass. Then Jake noticed a wooden table, on top of which was a partially completed mosaic of broken bottle glass. Lily watched closely as Jake went to it.

Interesting pieces of painted broken Coke bottle glass had been glued onto a piece of old wood. The glass chunks were big and small, smooth and sharp, a fascinating juxtaposition of sizes and textures. Each shard had been painted with oils. A vivid though thoughtfully restrained palette of natural tones had been used. The painted glass was affixed to an aged piece of stained wood, about three feet across, probably broken off some decaying outbuilding. The glass was arranged in an imaginative pattern resembling a tree with impossibly bright fruit set against a strange background of a dark wavy sky. The light fruit set in relief against the darkness was improbable and evocative and even a little unsettling.

"This is beautiful," said Jake.

Lily could only nod in acceptance as Jake saw several more glass mosaics leaning against the table and wall. Intrigued, he walked over to them. Some of the pieces were small and did not portray anything recognizable. Others were larger, with whimsical depictions. All used rough-hewn materials—painted bottle shards on salvaged strips of barn wood and found timber—but in a deliberate and artistic way.

"This is *your* work?"

"Guilty."

"Lily, seriously, this is beautiful art."

"Oh, I'm not sure what it is exactly, but you certainly can't call it art. A lot of my parents' friends are big collectors, and this definitely does not fit the definition."

"Have they seen this?"

"My parents' friends?" Lily laughed. "Oh, sure, I can just see the Havertys and the Woodruffs hanging my broken Coke bottles up right next to their Renoirs."

"I don't know about your parents' friends, but I think people would love this. *I* love it."

"Yes, well, you're . . . different from everyone else I know. And that's a good thing."

"Who else has seen this?"

"Just you."

He took that in, wondering if this was the reason she took him here today. He looked hard at her. Until now, he thought he knew her entirely. He was wrong. There was a depth of soul to Lily Davis Woodward that he was certain no one knew, perhaps not even Lily herself, the kind of soul that creates stirring mosaics of bright glass, or moves someone to create fireworks to express how she makes him feel. Looking back and forth between her vividly colored glass mosaics and her keen eyes, he felt as though he was getting a glimpse into those depths. And he wanted more. He wanted to go deeper.

"I think you're underestimating yourself."

"You're sweet, Jake, but trust me, breaking Coke bottles is not considered art around here. In fact, it's heresy. Which is precisely why I started doing it."

Lily explained how she first started sneaking off to the cabin as a child when something had made her angry. In defiance of her parents, she would come out here and smash the bottles in the fireplace. She'd smile politely on Doyle Street and "yes, ma'am" her way through a tea and nod gracefully to the ladies who lunched at the club, and then she'd come out here in her cabin in the kudzu in the woods and express her rage at the rules and rituals by throwing those holy bottles, smashing them up as she sometimes wanted to do to the world. Defaming the sanctified Coca-Cola Company was certain blasphemy in Toccoa, and on more than one occasion Lily would whip a few bottles into the stone fireplace and then genuflect and curtsy to the broken pieces while giggling aloud the radio jingle "Drink Coca-Cola!" as though she were snubbing her nose at society and all that it expected of her. If there was a hell, she sometimes wondered if this was the sort of thing that sent a girl there. Still, such concerns did not stop Lily Davis and now Lily Davis Woodward from her acts of desecration, which, perhaps in an even bigger snub, she turned into a secret art.

In adolescent years, before marriage, she came out here with oil paints. When her mother gave her an extravagant gown for a birthday instead of the paints she had begged for, Lily used her own money that she had saved to buy them. The heat and humidity eventually got to them, but she recently bought herself some new ones, even better colors, the ones in the glass jar in the mini-cellar.

Lily watched as Jake took in her secret. She had thought many times about bringing Paul out here but was never quite sure how he would respond. What would he think of someone who enjoyed smashing up his beloved company? What would he think of her hiding out by herself in the woods? What would he think of her art? Lily never quite knew, and when she was completely honest with herself, as she was right now, she delighted in having something just for herself, a secret of her own. But she also had to admit that she was even more thrilled to be sharing it with this man whom she had met. And she felt amazingly safe doing so.

Jake looked around, silently under-standing how important this place was in her life, how it was a part of her about which she chose not to tell, dared not tell, anyone, not even her husband. Jake nod-ded in that knowing way of his that made his grasp of complex emotions apparent, and she felt an unexpected and powerful bond with him, because he knew, he un-derstood from his sensitivity as well as his *own* experiences, how feelings could ex-plode and fuel a person's need to act and create. She saw in his gaze the belief that he had found more than a friend in her but also a like-minded traveler, a kindred soul. The protective shroud Jake had carried around him when they first met, that layer of aloneness, seemed to have faded, his

eyes bright and exposed and fully engaged with hers.

She picked up one of the bottles from
the floor, put it in a small burlap sack once
used to hold coffee beans, and pulled the
sack shut with its sewn-in tie.

"I don't care what kind of day you've
had, this is the best medicine in the world,"
she said.

Then she pulled back her arm and, as
hard as she could, threw the sack with the
bottle into the fireplace. It hit the big stones
in the back of the firebox and the bottle
shattered.

Lily laughed.

She marched up to the fireplace and
retrieved the sack, the broken glass inside
jangling as she walked back. She looked
exhilarated.

"Wanna try?" she said to Jake, her eyes
wide with joy.

"Sure."

She opened the sack and dumped the
new shards onto the pile of broken glass.
She put another bottle into the sack and
pulled the tie closed. Then she tossed the
sack to Jake, who caught it expertly.

"Go ahead, let 'er rip." She walked over

and stood next to him. He glanced at her and they shared a smile. This was fun.

As hard as he could, Jake threw the sack into the firebox. It hit the stones and shattered explosively.

Jake let out a little shout, but not as loud as Lily's. She loved this. After all these years of doing this alone, of coming out here alone, of being alone, Lily was overcome with the joy of sharing everything . . . throwing bottles and her glass mosaics and her kudzu cabin and her forest and her secrets and dreams . . . sharing everything with another person, with the right person, with Jake Russo. It was all so exciting and new.

They laughed together, close to each other. His face near. And his lips touched hers. There was no forethought. It was as natural as breathing. His lips stayed on hers and hers on his. And they kissed.

Their laughter stopped and they continued to kiss.

After a moment, they paused.

She looked into his eyes and in that moment with that look they said everything to each other. Slowly, he leaned into her again. Thoughts raced through her mind, but to utter them now would be like talking to a river.

He put his lips on hers and kissed her again. Slowly. Softly. At once exploring her and reaching out to her. He brought his hand to her and touched her face. He ran his open fingers through her hair, grazing the top of her ear, cradling the back of her head. Impulsively he pulled her closer and kissed her deeper.

A rush of new warmth spread through her and her heart went mad and her breath quickened. He heard her and it made him tremble.

He pulled his mouth off hers, put both hands on her face, and willed himself to take in a long, steadying breath.

Then he put his forehead on hers and took in the scent of her and the sound of her. Gently, barely making contact, his face slid down hers, his nose touching her eyelid, grazing her hairline, crossing and lingering against her ear and moving even slower down her jawline. His lips made the slightest contact with her skin and he stopped and began to kiss her neck.

He savored her, though he was afraid that at any moment something inside him would become abruptly unfastened and he would pour into her and tear into her and rip the world apart. His heart pounded completely unrestrained.

She felt him shaking as he touched her. She continued standing there, as if in a dream, and allowed herself to be savored. She felt at once both vulnerable and excited and let him explore her and take her in until she just couldn't stand it any longer.

She moaned, low and involuntary, and grabbed his head and pulled him up and kissed him. Her tongue in his mouth, they kissed passionately without reflection. Without consideration. Restraint gone. Never in her entire life had she ever been more certain of the rightness of a thing than this moment right now.

He ran both hands down her neck, slowly unbuttoned her dress, and slid it down and off her. He tugged the thin straps of her slip off her shoulders and ran his hands over the exposed skin of her upper back. She leaned into him and her slip fell to the ground.

He wrapped his arms around her back and pressed his face to her chest and ran his cheek down her body, his hands behind her, stopping at her belly to kiss her there and take her in there until neither of them could endure this one second longer.

Lifting her up, he gathered her into his arms and he kissed her again, more intensely, as he carried her to the blankets that he kicked open on the floor, and he laid her down on top of them and began to devour her.

He removed his shirt and ran his chest across her. The living swathe around the cabin made the midsummer air seem damp and heavy, and their bodies warmed it further. He reached for her bra, but she had already removed it. She lifted her hips so he could slide her underwear down her legs and off her. Like a stream coursing over her body, he seemed to be everywhere on her at once, kissing her breasts, his hands on them, his lips moving down her stomach again, his fingers rising to her neck and to her mouth, his tongue moving across her. Seeking, caressing, his hands ran all over her with a rising urgency, slipping over her and down her, exploring her, his fingers in her, his mouth on her, his tongue in her.

She cried out and it could have ended

there for her, but he kept going, losing himself in her.

He wanted to know every piece of her, all her secrets, everything she hid from the world, what gave her pleasure. He wanted every single part of her body and spirit, and he wanted to at once both have her and consume her.

She lay there as he knelt over her and quickly removed his belt and pants, and for a brief moment in a diaphanous column of light she saw all of him, this man whom she had met in a field yesterday. Then he leaned over and put himself on her and then, slowly, into her.

She rooted her fingers into his upper back, his muscles hard and expansive as he held his weight above her. His chest rubbing lightly against her breasts, his abdomen on her belly, their fevering bodies sliding together skin to skin, his kissing and touching and holding enveloping her to where she was wrapped in him, suffused in him, it was dizzying, overwhelming, and now to be filled with him, feel him simultaneously moving in her and all around her, sense him touching all parts of her, body and beyond, the rising swirl of sensations and emotions brought her to a threshold and she began to cry, partly from the pleasure of it and partly from what the pleasure was setting into relief, the juxtaposition of what she had and what she hadn't had, in all ways, in all ways possible.

He didn't ask her why she was crying and she didn't try to explain. He knew exactly why, and she knew that he knew.

He continued making love to her, kissing her tears, and she realized that this right now was inevitable. When she had been dancing alone, this was who she was with. When she had imaginary partners, this was who she had imagined. And from the moment she saw his firework exploding in the sky over her house the die was cast. His fireworks were calling to her, leading her to this, and if she wasn't here right now with him she felt as though she would be dead.

He pulled her up. She sat on him and they held each other like that, still as one, both quivering. They kissed, ran their hands tenderly down the entire lengths of each other's arms and sides and backs, and looked into each other. In her hazy eyes he could see that he was not alone, as he had felt for so long. He held her face, adoringly, lovingly, and kissed her eyelids. Spellbound, he stroked her hair, drawing it away as if to open her further, reveal another layer of her, and then pulling her close, her chin moving back and upward, mouth open with the bliss, and he kissed her softly, lips moist, hot-breathed, all along her throat and neck, mesmerized, almost pained, by how delicate and exquisite a thing she was.

They stayed like this for a long time, hugging, until, ever so slightly, she began to move her hips. She felt herself swelling and then tightening on him again, a flushing spreading as her blood heated, and she found herself uttering words and sounds entirely involuntarily, and she gave in to this, tossing aside control in a way she never thought she could or would, and finally, when he could not remain still any longer on this plateau, he shoved her over and he pushed her knees back toward her and he fell, and rose and fell, with her, arms before him, reaching for her, needing her, casting off his contained self, with its quiet and damage, and connecting with her, fully and deeply and entirely, leaving behind the remains of restraint and giving in to the building rhythm of human bond.

They locked eyes. He was so beautiful like that, she thought. She watched him as he moved over her and with her, his hand on her cheek, on her breasts, on her face again, cradling it, and he was whispering to her as though she were the most important thing that had ever been and would ever be, and she thought about the way he had covered her body with his in the field that very first time and touched her leg and blown on her knee, and the way he made coffee and cooked and drank wine, and now he was focusing all of that passion onto and into her, sating her entire body and soul with it, and with his release imminent there was more fullness, and she again began contractions, wet spasms, waves rippling through every part of her in still greater implausible ways, words again rushing forth wildly, mixing with his, responding to his, her hands gripping his shoulders and arms, an open palm sliding and slipping along his back as she felt like she was being gently but powerfully taken to some place that she had never before been, the Spanish moss parting like a velvet curtain when she was eight years old and the vast and improbable ocean before her for the first time, and she was nine and a half in her backyard looking up wide-eyed at the fireworks, exploding in ways that she now felt and shared and saw in Jake's eyes above, taking her beyond the bounds of home, beyond everything she knew and understood, taking her away from Toccoa, away from this world, and bringing her to a place where she was only her bare and true self.

There was no lasting resolution to their lovemaking but pauses through the night, when breathing slowed, sweat-soaked hair was wiped tenderly from faces, soft kisses exchanged, sweet words murmured, as they lay in each other's arms before beginning again, hours pouring into hours.

Enwrapped in this closeness so completely, cocooned by it, Lily knew that this was what had been missing from her life, this feeling of wholeness and connection, fulfillment of her capacity to share the entirety of herself with all of another. This man. She knew it with the same force of nature flowing through any spent creature slumbering in its silk. And now that she had found it, and him, how could she go back to her life as it was?

She took comfort in knowing that at least for a little while longer she didn't have to think about it.

Lily lay back in Jake's arms looking at the timbered roof overhead, planks and beams smooth and worn, antiqued by a century of summers, and she noticed a small hole, charred neatly around its rim as though some piece of a thing from far beyond had come flaming, crashing neatly through the roof as if marking her cabin had been its calling. Somehow, the discovery moved her. Although she had no way of knowing that the hole was in fact made by an errant piece of the fireworks shot over Bartam's Field on July 4th eleven years ago, the fireworks that she saw from her parents' house, she knew, somewhere, that there was an order and a purpose that defied the gravity of reason and joined faraway things together. But Lily didn't

think about all that now. She made an effort not to think about much at all but just
to absorb the feelings around her, allowing
herself to be swept away in her lover's
arms.

LILY'S STAR

A whitetail buck browsed through the vines in the darkness outside the cabin and then moved on. Inside, pools of blue-green moonlight rippled along the floor and walls.

"Do you think if we lie here long enough the kudzu will come get us?" Jake wondered aloud. He lay on his back while Lily, spooned against him and propped up on an elbow, fed him corn soufflé with her fingers.

"Fear not, my darling. I will protect you."

"Thank you. That gives me great comfort, O killer of the vine."

"You don't kill the kudzu. You can't kill the kudzu. It's like the moon and the stars. It is always there. You see, you have to make peace with kudzu."

"I see. Befriend the vine."

"Exactly."

"You are wise beyond your years."

Jake sucked soufflé off her fingers and kissed playfully up her arms, rapt with the scent and softness of her ruddy, glowing skin. She smiled teasingly and rolled atop him, continuing to feed him the sweet corn pudding and kissing him, first on his face, then his neck, and slowly along his chest.

"You realize you are going to kill me!" he exclaimed.

"Yes, but, mmm . . . what a way to go," she said mischievously between kisses, her lips moving unhurriedly across his taut belly, moisture from her tongue lingering on him as she spoke. "They found them, surrounded by a mass of vines which had climbed on everything in sight—"

"—except, strangely and inexplicably, it had not touched their decomposing bodies. Because they had 'befriended the vine.'"

Lily laughed as she kissed his body.

Jake loved this playful, fun, curious side of her, but where was she finding this stamina? he wondered. She seemed to be making up for all the time they had not been together like this. Trying to wrap the past, and perhaps the future, into the here and now. What she was doing now did something to him, and he gave himself over to her.

He stroked her hair as she came across a deep scar that started on his side, just above his hip bone. She stopped and traced the scar, which became deeper and broader across his lower back.

He pulled away a little and she could feel the entire tone change. She had stumbled across a ghost, and her touch had conjured the apparition. She knew instantly not to ask about it, but at the same time her lack of words left a void that promised to engulf this precious and newfound thing between them that he did not want to go. Jake lay back, and after a long moment, he spoke again.

"People listen to the reporters and they read the papers and they see the newsreels, but they don't understand. They can't. War is a private experience. And the longer you're at it and the more you see, and the more you do . . ." Jake's voice cracked ever so slightly. He paused for a moment, then continued, "The more private an experience it becomes."

For the first time, Lily got a glimpse into what Jake Russo had been through, what had hurt him so deeply and caused him to wander cross-country without home or community. More than anything she wanted to soothe that pain, kiss away the anguish, but she dare not approach that place. She dare not battle an apparition she could not see or touch or know. So she remained silent and let instinct take over once again, running her hands through his hair. He liked that. His body was so responsive to her touch, so sensual. Could you love someone you'd known for barely one day? What if you felt that you'd known that person your whole life, even though you just met him?

"You can share anything with me, Jake. Even that," she said as gently as a person possibly could.

Jake inhaled deeply and closed his eyes. What could he say to her? *I am sharing everything with you*, he thought.

Every time my chest expands with breath against yours, every time my heart beats in tempo with yours, I am sharing everything. How could he make her understand? He opened his eyes. "You asked me when we had dinner in the field if I had changed," he said. "What I've come to believe is that you have to cherish . . . this, the present. Life and death . . . it's a matter of a breath, a heartbeat . . . a single footstep." He thought about Lorena, who had stepped on a mine in her vineyard, and he held Lily even tighter thinking about the simple timing of things. He had seen so much that was arbitrary—things you couldn't make sense of, let alone try to explain with words. He held her even tighter and tried to convey these thoughts with the stroke of his hands, the pound of his pulse, tried to pass them to her through his touch. "This, the here and the now, Lily, this is what you count on."

"I lost my brother in the war," she said evenly.

He sat up, a little taken aback by this. "You didn't tell me."

"I'm telling you. His name was Jonathan. He was a paratrooper in the Solomons. He was older than me and had his own life. I didn't know him all that well, but I loved him very much. Everyone did. He had that effect on people, especially my parents. They don't talk about him much. My mother doesn't talk about him at all."

Jake took this in, watching her, evaluating, seeing the pain that she kept away. He understood, perhaps in a way no one else Lily knew ever could, that her brother was more in her life now than he was when he was alive. Now Jake was the one who spoke gingerly.

"Ghosts are hard to live with," he said.

"Yes, Jake. They are." There was a long moment of understanding between them. "Sometimes I wonder . . . why him? You know? Was someone aiming at him or did he just step the wrong way for a second? Sometimes I wonder if I had used rayon instead of silk for my wedding dress, would there have been one more parachute for one more soldier to jump out of that plane with him and save his life?"

"I know those thoughts."

"I know you do."

She pulled him close again and they

smiled at each other, a hundred lifetimes of expressions exchanged with that look. He had never thought he would be alive like this again, and now he had found someone not only whom he allowed near but who truly understood him, who was truly with him. She had always thought this kind of closeness was just a dream, but in an instant he had shown her that such fancies were real—but how much did all this matter? She had already given herself away. Yes, in this life, so much was arbitrary and timing was everything.

Lily found herself wondering what would have happened if she had never gotten out of her car to walk into that field and never met Jake Russo. What if the arbitrary winds had sent a friend walking to her on Doyle Street, delaying her and keeping her from seeing the firework? What if a deer had crossed the road, causing Lily to slow or stop her car for a few moments? What if she just never looked up? She would have lived out her days with . . . what? A feeling that something was missing. A sense of longing. Temptation never acted upon. Would that really have been a fate so terrible? Wasn't that how so many people lived their lives?

Because now that she knew what this was, what exactly had been missing, and how it had rushed into the void she had felt, how could she now unfill it? How could you empty a great natural lake? How could she ever extract Jake Russo from the emptiness that had once been her soul? And if she could not—and if she could not be with him, which of course was even more impossible than forgetting him—how could she live the rest of her days with such a weight, such a voluminous thing that most certainly would turn heavier with each minute he was gone and bluer with each hour he was not holding her until finally, unbearable, it pulled her down? To think about it, even for a brief pained moment, was to fall into a chasm, to lose herself in the deepest of trenches, spirit bubbling out of her in silent screams, where she would be physically present but otherwise gone from those around her, those in her life, Paul. Like some limp rag doll, she would be in attendance, taken along, smiling, but that wouldn't be her. She wouldn't really be there, and they would never find her. They might as well dredge the ocean for a trinket.

Sensing her inner turmoil, Jake held Lily tightly and kissed her on the forehead, and her doubts were instantly allayed. She smiled and hugged him back. No, she thought, looking at him, feeling his arms around her, no, she would rather have a few days of this and know what it was than spend the rest of her life standing on a porch, looking out at the sky, a cocktail in her hand, dressed up and empty, made up and lost, just like so many people she had seen at her parents' parties, just like so many in Toccoa. No, she would rather be underwater with her eyes open than aboveground, a phantom of a woman in a soulless world.

Being here with this man right now, she was certain that she had never been happier and more fulfilled in her life. But was this really all there was to that, Lily thought further, the here and now, as he had said? How could it be? How could there not be something beyond this moment to how she felt? She took in the beating of his heart, as he had told her, listened to his breath, as he had directed, sensed the currents running through the fibers of his flesh, and looked into his eyes—chance be damned! How could what they had in each other's arms, the infinity of emotion they saw when they looked into each other, soon be banished to the confines of memory just because of the simple timing of things? Was the world really and truly so cruel that it would taunt the spirit with such joy and then rip it away a few days later because of temporal matters? And even if so possessed, was it even capable? Could what they had really be cast aside even if *they* tried to do so?

Although logic told Lily otherwise, the whispering in the breeze through the kudzu said surely there must be some plan that could not yet be seen. Like hearing laughter in a stream, she wanted to believe.

He hugged her tightly. While doing so, he came across a small scar on her shoulder. He touched it, giving her a questioning look.

"You want to hear *my* war story?" she said, changing the tone of their conversation with a little playfulness.

"I do," he said.

Lily took a deep breath, then decided to tell him. "I was babysitting my little cousin, Margie, and we came across a bear, not far from here actually."

"Really?" Jake said, with eyebrows raised. "A bear?"

"Yes, oh yes, he was huge, ferocious, a massive grizzly, and very hungry, yes, and he was trying to get at our picnic which we'd just set out and I'm sorry, but there was no way I was gonna give up a freshly baked pecan pie without a fight, so I picked up this long sycamore branch and I—"

He began to smile. "Lily, as far as I know, there are no grizzly bears in Georgia."

Lily couldn't suppress her laugh. "Right. Well, actually, I was chasing Margie around the living room with a pillow and I slipped and hit an end table. Broke my mother's lamp, and trust me—a grizzly would've been preferable."

Jake laughed. "A sycamore branch? You're bad."

"I know. I'm sorry."

"Hey, as far as I'm concerned, anyone who makes corn soufflé this good can say or do anything she wants."

"Anything?"

"Anything."

She rolled onto him and they laughed together and began to kiss again.

Dawn, July 2, 1945

Lily opened her eyes, the new day awash in gossamer light, to find Jake Russo in her secret cabin, sitting across from her, writing in his moleskin journal. He had lit a small fire in the fireplace sometime in the night, which made the cabin very cozy.

"You don't happen to have any of that great coffee of yours around, do you?" She smiled and yawned.

"Oh, how I wish."

"You're not drawing a picture of me sleeping with drool coming out of my mouth, are you?"

"Thought about it, but no. Something else."

Lily got up and went to him, watching him work. He was writing something, which was not in English. It was in a language that posters in the Toccoa Post Office called "the language of the enemy."

"Practicing your Italian?" she asked lightly.

Without looking up, Jake smiled. In careful, precise handwriting, he had written something out in Italian, what looked like verses of poetry. Then Lily saw that Jake was writing the title at the top. It read: LA STELLA DI LILY. "I've never been much of a poet or a painter and I can't buy you a fancy gift," he said with a smile. "This is the best that I can do for you. It's a very special firework, Lily. A great blue one. True deep blue, like your eyes, is the rarest of all pyrotechnic colors. Very few Americans have ever seen a real blue firework. Even in Italy, it is rare. There are only a few families that know how to do it. Centuries ago, my family learned how to distill this wonderful material, magnalium, and use a composite of it in the formula. It is a difficult and laborious process. For years, the men in my family have made variations of the blue firework. My great-grandfather made a 'blue,' still talked about in Naples, called 'La Stella di Contessa.' My great-grandmother was Contessa. I updated it a bit with some things I learned."

He very carefully tore the page out of the journal and handed it to Lily.

Lily read the title. "'La Stella di Lily.'"

"Lily's Star. I figure, everyone deserves their own star."

Looking over the beautiful words as her hands held the paper before her, Lily was overcome with emotion. This was the most romantic gesture she had ever encountered. She opened her mouth but was speechless. As if its words could seep into her and pump through her, she pulled the paper to her chest, and she felt a force, that connection to others, a link to links through time and space and centuries of rare passion, something whose truth lived beyond the fibers of the paper and the ties of the present.

"Jake, I . . . I don't know what to say."

"Say you'll see me again today."

This was insane, she knew that. Her husband was returning in two days. There were a million reasons why she had to end this, but as she looked at the paper in her hand she didn't want to think about anything except Jake Russo.

"I'd love to see you later today."

"Early afternoon again?"

"Yes."

"Good."

"You know this is crazy."

"Not seeing you is crazier."

They began to get ready to go. Jake threw on his jeans and started straightening up the cabin. But he couldn't seem to take his eyes off Lily. He watched hypnotically as she gathered her clothing. The way she moved, carried herself, her hair shimmering in the sunlight, the depth of expression across her lovely face when lost in her own thoughts, the perfect curves of her body, oh, the curves of her body, excruciating not to reach out and trace with his touch. She was breathtaking, Jake thought, simply breathtaking.

Jake continued watching her as she put on her clothes and did the best she could to smooth her hair out with her hands and fingers. It was these little ordinary things, subtleties of women that drove men crazy, that both tantalized and allured. And now, the way Lily tossed her hair back. Buttoned her dress. Slipped her foot into a sandal. It was carnal, bewitching, watching her engaged in the simple routine of her life. Jake committed the images of her to long-term memory, his mind reeling, wondering what it would be like to see her every day, to be part of these private moments first thing every morning, to share the conversations and intimacies of two people living their lives together every night before sleep.

She caught him staring at her.

"What?"

"You're beautiful, Lily."

She smiled back at him, looking away for a moment as all his attention rushed over her. Feeling flattered, cherished, and so close to him, she finished dressing as he watched. Then she turned and looked at him intently.

"Last night, I remembered something," she said. "When I was nine and a half years old, I saw fireworks, amazing fireworks, from the backyard at my parents' house, and I remember having this incredible sense of not just how beautiful and magnificent they were, but how they made me feel, expansive and open and capable, I really think, of sharing everything big and small, all that the world has to offer, with another person. It was the first time I got a glimpse into the depths of who I was, who

I am. Someone with me, my father, I think, told me never to forget how I felt, that wonder and sense of possibility, but I guess as I got older, I don't know, it kind of faded into the background, chalked up as some silly childhood memory, and I never saw fireworks again. Until you."

Lily took his hands and gathered her thoughts, continuing. "Jake, meeting you has made me feel the way I did when I was that child, and no matter what, I never want to lose that again."

He kissed her, and in an instant it made his insides swim. He put his cheek on hers, to feel her skin on his once again. Closing his eyes, he ran his fingers through her hair, still dampish, taking her in with all his senses. Her sweat was a potion, her scent elixir.

She kissed him back.

Getting ready to go, they made sure the fire, where they had burned the paper sack and wax paper, was completely extinguished. Before they left, she put the journal paper he had given her in the glass jar with her paints, her other prized possessions.

He watched her screw the metal top back on the jar. She was right, of course. This was crazy. He'd just given his heart to someone who was hiding it under a board in the floor. But where else was she going to keep it? Where else could she hide her secrets? He didn't want to think about that. He didn't want to think about two days from now. He just wanted to think about when he would be with her next. That thick shell he had developed, the guardedness that had kept him from being close to people, that had sent him on the road, had dissolved like the morning mist in the heat of the sun. He could feel it. And for Jake Russo, Lily Davis Woodward was the sun.

Lily pulled the Packard up the driveway, parked, and got out. The eastern sky was already bright and honeyed with new day. She strolled up to the house feeling a little like she was drunk. Her hair was a mess. Her dress dirty and disheveled. And she looked as though she had never been more radiant in her entire life. She hummed a little to herself, one of the songs she'd heard in that night in the field.

Lily bounded up the back stairs and into the kitchen and immediately realized that something was wrong. Something was very wrong. She looked around and it hit her. The boxes were gone. The entire mess was gone. She looked around and discovered that everything had been unpacked and her entire kitchen was set up.

She ran into the foyer and saw that the boxes that had been there were now also gone, their contents unpacked.

She swung her head into the living room and was immediately startled by the man sitting on her sofa.

"Daddy!"

"Good morning, Lily," said Walter Davis.

THE BRIGHT LIGHT OF DAY

What are you doing here?"

"I called you over and over, Lily," Walter Davis said. He stood, which was something that had a powerful effect in a room.

Lily remained silent and walked toward him, feeling smaller with every step.

"Then Havis Brown called me yesterday," he continued. "Said he'd seen the Packard by the side of Owl Swamp Road, over by Bartam's Field. I got concerned and left Atlanta early."

Lily remembered she'd seen the Browns' pickup drive by and slow when she was with Jake in the field, when he was tending to her knee. She also remembered that Lilah Brown was active with the Ladies Auxiliary. The Browns were such busybodies, she thought. Lily paced the living room, looking around, while her father stood calmly.

"You cleaned everything?" she said nervously.

"Everything needed to be cleaned." Walter Davis paused for a moment, then looked hard at his daughter. "I've been here all night, honey."

There was another long moment between them. She knew very well what he was saying to her. As always, her father quietly knew everything. She felt a distressing mixture of guilt and sadness, like she had let her father down, but also regret that she couldn't share with him all the wonderful things she felt about this incredible man whom she had met. Perhaps saddest of all, Lily felt, was that Walter would have liked Jake. He would have liked Jake a great deal, even though Jake was Italian, of that she was sure.

But this wasn't one of their camping trips from her childhood, where they talked openly and freely about whatever came to mind, sparks from a fire crackling before them through the night. No, those days were gone. Though Lily felt fairly sure that both she and her father were still essentially the same—this was still the man who would come home from a trip and throw down his jacket and roll up his sleeves and shampoo his little girl's hair in the tub and then talk to her for an hour about his travels and her dreams while she sat in the warm water—everything around them had changed.

"And there's something else," he continued. "Paul got himself onto an earlier plane. He will be home tomorrow."

Lily took that in. Walter watched as she was hit with a tidal wave of mixed emotions.

"Does Mother—"

"Your mother knows he's coming home early, and she'll be back from Atlanta tonight. But she doesn't know why I left early for Toccoa. I told her I had to leave yesterday to get some sales figures I'd left at home for the London office. As you know, some things are best kept from your mother. I don't like lying, Lily. But I also understand that sometimes people do what they need to do."

Lily nodded, sensing that he was talking about her.

"Sit down, honey," Walter Davis said gently.

Lily acquiesced, sitting back straight, knees together, as though polite posture could somehow distract from the disheveled mess she knew she was, a girl who had been out all night in the woods with a boy.

Walter paced for a moment as though he were in a boardroom, thinking, pondering her life with the same acumen and weight he gave to multinational business decisions affecting tens of thousands of employees. Then he walked over and sat down next to her, leaning in close as if to comfort her. She could smell the sweet scent of perique, the expensive tobacco that her father always smoked in his pipes. When she was a child, she always knew he'd been in to check on her when she'd awake in the night and smell that sweet scent in her room. That scent always soothed her.

"Lily, if you had come to me and asked what I thought three years ago, I would have told you that I thought you were too young to get married."

Lily was surprised. "Daddy, I had no idea that you—"

"Let me talk," he cut her off, and she shut her mouth. "I would have told you not to do it. But you didn't ask. And your mother . . . well, you know what she thought. So I let her speak for both of us, as you know I often do."

Lily was shocked to hear this. But as the information sunk in and she thought about her father's muted reactions to her wedding, it made sense to her.

"When I was in law school," he said, continuing, "before I met your mother, I dated. I had 'flings.' I had what you might call a pre-adulthood. You did not have any of that. Your childhood was stunted, just like much of the world the last three years. But all that is over now."

"Daddy—" Lily had never heard her father speak to her like this.

"No. Listen. Three years ago you did not come to me and ask what I thought, and even if you did and I had told you,

you wouldn't have listened to me. Well, you listen to me now. You are not asking, but I am telling and you will listen. You are beautiful and smart, Lilybelle, and as far as I'm concerned the most tenacious person I have ever met. You got that from your mother and I swear you are more obstinate than her. But you are an adult now. And that means you have responsibilities."

"I love Paul, I do, Daddy, but—"

"The last few years the entire world has been upside down, and due to great sacrifice it's been made right again. Don't talk to me about love. I know all about love. From the first moment I held you in my arms I loved you so deeply you can't even begin to comprehend it, and I know I don't tell you that enough, but there you have it. You mean everything to me, but you are an adult now and it's time to start acting like one. Sixty million people died, Lily. Half a million Americans, including your brother. To change the world. To make it a better place. Not because it was easy or because it felt right, not because of love. They did it out of a sense of selflessness, out of a sense of duty."

"Daddy, I just don't—"

"Stop. Don't talk. Just be quiet." Walter Davis rarely raised his voice above an even pitch, but when he did, as he did now for a brief moment, it silenced senators, stopped dictators mid-sentence, and could bring tears to the eyes of his daughter. Lily wrung her hands. Nothing could get to her like the idea that she had disappointed her father.

"The world is now right and it will stay that way." He leaned in even closer to her. "I have been married to the same woman at least five times. Marriage comes in phases. Some good, some not so good. But you work through things, and you grow, and you change, and you stick by the decisions that you made, even when you were seventeen. That is your duty."

Walter Davis rose. Lily stayed silent.

"Now, your mother will be at our house at noon. We are entertaining the Woodwards this evening, who will be coming up from Gainesville this afternoon. I'd like you to come early and greet them, and help your mother and GiGi prepare supper. Your house is ready for tomorrow. I'd like you to be, too. I love you so, Lily."

Walter Davis kissed her on the head and walked out.

"Have you ever seen Toccoa, Georgia, look so bright and happy?" exclaimed Honey.

"No, Mother. I can't say I have."

Honey drove Walter's 1942 Cadillac sedan, the huge company car, down Doyle Street through the center of town. Though the chrome had been painted per "black-out" orders from Washington, like all of the few cars still delivered after December 1941, the Davis sedan was quite a sight. On Honey's request, Mrs. Keener had slaughtered an eighteen-pound goose that morning, one of several that had been fattened for years on the grass in her peach orchard. Lily accompanied Honey downtown to pick up the bird, which would be the main course of their evening meal with the Woodwards.

The sidewalks were jammed with people and it seemed that nearly all of them looked up and smiled and offered a greeting when they saw the big Caddy cruising down Doyle. Honey and Lily found their smiles, as they always did, and waved back. Coming downtown alone was one thing. Coming downtown with Honey was like accompanying a duchess. Lily's arm often hurt from all the waving. They parked the car and got out. Lily took a deep breath, making sure her downtown face was suitably applied.

Immediately folks began to greet them and wave to them, and of course Lily and Honey greeted them and waved back with an effortless rhythm, in perfect harmony with each other, as though they had spent months practicing. They walked by Barron's Drugs, packed with people young and old, all gathered around the soda fountain. Tobacco-chewing men in blue overalls at Ralph Wilson's Feed & Seed, who'd come from all over the county to discuss the fine points of manure, stopped their conversation and waved respectfully as the Davis women walked by. At a corner, Lily and Honey could see up the street dozens of rockers moving like pistons all along the wide Victorian-style porch on Mamy Simmons' mansion, which was flooded with guests, mint juleps in many hands, "white lightning" and OJ in others. Continuing along Doyle, Honey and her daughter approached the Ritz movie theater, where Lily had kissed Paul throughout much of *The Maltese Falcon* without ever taking her eyes off the screen. Its marquee read: WELCOME HOME, BOYS.

Women from the Daughters of the American Revolution, the Down to Earth Garden Club, the Civitan Club, the United Daughters of the Confederacy, and the Ladies Auxiliary of Toccoa had descended on the town, decorating lampposts and storefronts and Confederate monuments in front of city buildings for the homecoming celebration.

Someone had wheeled an upright piano out onto the sidewalk under the Ritz marquee, and a young sailor was playing a very up-tempo version of Johnny Mercer and Ziggy Elman's "And the Angels Sing." Several people passing by, some in uniform, some townsfolk, joined him and started singing. A few started swing dancing. Another sailor produced a bugle and joined in the impromptu celebration right on the sidewalk in the center of Doyle Street. "We meet, and the angels sing. The angels sing the sweetest song I ever heard. You speak, and the angels sing. Or am I breathing music into every word."

It became impossible to ignore this joy that was spreading across town like the scent of the sweet-tomato barbeque sauce pouring from steel barrel grills. A returning soldier and his date started dancing on the sidewalk, too. Soon a few more couples joined them. Lily watched with Honey as a young Army officer took the hand of a gleeful local girl as the impromptu dancing grew and poured over into the street. "You smile, and the angels sing. And though it's just a gentle murmur at the start. We kiss, and the angels sing. And leave their music ringing in my heart."

Even a lady of society like Honey Davis had to smile at the goings-on downtown. Such manners would normally be derided as the conduct of bohemians and pinup girls, and, certainly, dancing under the movie marquee was not typical behavior for Toccoa. But these were not typical days.

"Hi, Mrs. Davis."

"Hello, Mrs. Davis."

"Afternoon, Mrs. Davis."

Hats were tipped as Honey and Lily

walked by and returned the joyous greetings. Just as they were approaching Keener's Market, someone came jogging at Lily from the crowd on the street.

"Lily?"

She turned at the sound of her name being called.

"Lily!"

An exuberant and very pregnant young woman waddled over and threw her arms around Lily, barely giving her a chance to breathe.

"Oh, look at you, Lils! How are you?"

"Hi, Jenna."

"You look fabulous."

"And you look—"

"Twins! Can you believe it?! Ahh!"

The young woman patted her massive belly, radiating joy. A young man in a wheelchair joined her.

"Hello, Lily," he said.

"Hello, Mark."

He wheeled himself over, next to his pregnant spouse. The deep and whimsical smiles he and Lily exchanged were not lost on Honey.

"Mrs. Davis," the young man said, nodding a respectful greeting to Honey.

The young man was pensive, contained, his carelessly rumpled hair a stark contrast to his brightly dressed and ebullient wife.

"It's nice to see you home, Mark," said Honey.

Mark nodded but seemed to bristle uncomfortably in his chair.

"We simply couldn't miss the homecoming," Jenna said. "Oh, it's just so wonderful to see everyone!"

"I know your parents are happy to see you. Your mother fills me in on all your exciting news every time I see her at the club. How are things in San Francisco?"

"Sausalito," Mark said.

"Oh," said Honey, unable to hide that she was misinformed. "How are things in Sausalito?"

"It's really quite an interesting town. Just across the bay from the city. The shipbuilding has stopped for the most part," Jenna said.

"A lot of artists are starting to move there," said Mark.

"And you're working for a paper, I understand?" Honey prompted.

"A news agency."

"He's a reporter," Jenna said.

"Well, something like that." "Reporter" sounded more exciting to many people than the reality, which was sitting behind a desk and fact-checking news before it went out over the wires.

"We thought it was important for us to, you know, strike out on our own," Jenna said. "While we're young."

Honey knew that the young couple had been under a lot of pressure to work for Jenna's family's business, but they were resistant to the idea, Mark apparently more so than Jenna. Her family owned one of Toccoa's most successful firms, a casket company. The manufacturer had prospered for decades, but business during the last few years had never been better. In 1942, the casket company had removed its signage so that it was no longer visible from Route 123, the road from the train depot to Camp Toccoa, traveled by new soldiers when they arrived in town for training before being sent to the battlefield.

"I was so sorry to hear about your brother," said Jenna.

"Thank you," Lily replied.

"I remember watching him play football when I was a little girl. He was so good."

"And your brother comes home on the Fourth?" asked Honey, changing the subject.

"Yes, he does. We're all so excited."

"That *is* exciting. Paul comes home tomorrow," said Honey.

"Oh. You must be positively jumping out of your skin," squealed Jenna, reaching out and squeezing Lily's hands. "Three and a half years he's been gone, right?"

"Three years, four months," said Lily.

"Wow." Jenna giggled, perhaps envisioning what a man and a woman do when reunited after so long.

"Are you still drawing, Mark?" Lily asked.

"Not so much. I've actually been doing some work with silhouettes."

"Silhouettes. How nice," said Honey.

"I know it's a little old-fashioned. Something I picked up while I was recovering in France."

"It's his little hobby, which he'll most likely have little time for very soon." Jenna smiled playfully, patted her belly, and kissed him.

"When are you leaving?" asked Lily.

"On the fifth," said Mark.

"Have to get back and get the nursery ready! Can you believe it? Twins! Ahh!" And Jenna gave Lily a kiss. "Despite a few bumps in the road, everything is turning out just like we always dreamed."

They said their good-byes and Jenna wheeled Mark off.

"You let us know when you're back with those babies, you hear?" Honey called out. "I want to be first in town to throw y'all a Sip 'n' See!"

Lily just watched them go, thinking it might be quite a long time before Honey got the chance to throw Jenna and her babies a shower. Jenna was one of Lily's best friends growing up. There were many. But seeing her now was jarring. Unsettling. In spite of Jenna's sentiment, everything was not turning out like they had always dreamed. There were no dreams of handsome, carefree Mark Morgan in a wheelchair. The lanky boy Lily once went swimming with, who drew her in charcoal while she lay drying in the sun in her underwear, who sat by her talking and laughing and skipping stones along the water one sweet and simple midsummer night.

No dreams of her brother shot dead in waist-high water off a beach on some South Pacific atoll. No dreams of marrying Paul Woodward and one day having an affair in a cabin in the woods, one day out of the blue realizing that her perfect marriage to a perfect boy was not the culmination of all her dreams but quite possibly the greatest mistake of her life.

Seeing Jenna put the past into relief, pointing out just how different it was from the present, just how different it was from what was planned and hoped. How different the present truly was from how it was expected to be. What could the future possibly hold next? What was to become of her life?

So the two watched as Jenna wheeled her husband down the sidewalk.

"That poor boy, bless his heart," said Honey. "He used to be so wild. Remember?"

"I remember."

"He still has a crush on you."

"Stop it, Mother."

"Well, he does. Anyone can see it. Plain as day. I don't know what it was with you and the wild boys. They all liked you."

"Mother."

"It's true and you know it. Well, I couldn't be happier for him and Jenna, running off to Sausalito and *all*. After what he went through in Normandy, twins. What a gift. What a blessing."

"Yes."

"Now I know you only had a few weeks, but with the slightest care and calculation, that's really all it takes."

"Excuse me?"

"Shoot for the middle of the month, dear. About ten days after. That's the time."

"Mother."

"Understand?"

Lily shut her eyes and willed herself to breathe in, and then out. Guidance regarding her reproductive cycle was perhaps the last thing Lily desired from her mother right now.

"Oh my lord," said Honey, looking at her watch. "We're late for our appointments." Honey grabbed her daughter's arm, urging her along.

"What appointments?"

"Come on, dear."

"I thought we were here to get a goose."

"We will. Right after."

"What appointments?"

Honey just smiled.

"Mother, I will tell you right now. I am not getting my hair done at Betty's."

"Really, Lily, you're such a contrarian. Tomato, tomahto. Your husband is returning from the war. Stop being such a stick-in-the-mud."

"I am not getting my hair done at Betty's."

Lily looked into the mirror at the wavy mass of hair gelled and pinned high above her forehead and the long rolling curls cascading down her shoulders. She coughed as a thick gob of heavily scented styling lotion was applied all around her head.

"Oh, Lily, you look just like Joan Crawford," Betty Lou Beasley declared.

"Paul's going to think he's come home to a Hollywood movie star," said Honey.

Honey sat next to her daughter in a chair, a helmet of setting lotion applied to her impeccable head as well. All around them a gaggle of very made-up ladies, the grooming of their glamorous waved and curled hair in various stages of completion, filled Betty Lou's Salon.

Lily understood the role of makeup and hairdos in a woman's life, particularly during a time of war. When so many women were working in the factories and fields she knew it was important to maintain a sense of femininity. Unlike her mother, she liked the soft, romantic look of her generation, long wavy locks pulled away from creamy powdered faces. But what some women went through for this look, Lily felt, was ridiculous. Femininity was one thing. Sleeping in steel curlers was another. And submitting to Betty Lou, that was even worse.

Many of the ladies at Betty's, which had not one vacant seat today, had been there for hours. Blondes, brunettes, and redheads sat in salon chairs while several white-coated beauticians worked on them, painstakingly, vigilantly, as if they were bombs on the assembly line. Meticulous rows of long pin curls were tightly wound and set with steel spring clips. Long locks forcefully parted and pulled around countless curlers, set and secured with nickel-plated bobby pins. Patriotic red lipstick and black mascara and layer upon layer of high-gloss fingernail polish exactingly applied. The room stunk of a sickeningly sweet concoction: hair tonic compounds, acetone, and Chanel N°5. And throughout it all, the ladies chattered and gossiped with the vibrancy of bees at the honeyflow.

"Birdie Trogdon Caudell was the most beautiful early spring bride."

"Oh, she was breathtaking."

"Breathtaking."

"And that dress."

"Oh. Full-length organza, Alençon lace yoke, cathedral train."

"Scandalously low neckline."

"And that baby. So cute."

"So cute."

"What baby?"

"Her baby."

"She's already had a baby? They were married in March."

"Yes, they were."

"Boy, I'll bet Johnny Caudell was surprised."

"Not as surprised as Birdie's fiancé, when he came back in April."

Lily just sat there, staring silently at herself in the mirror, yielding to Betty Lou's designs and feeling very much like a large poodle. This was the exact same mirror

Lily had looked into three-something years ago the day of her wedding when a brigade of beauticians and bridesmaids fussed and flitted about her like dwarves and forest creatures in a Disney movie. How odd, she remembered thinking even then, all the layers and coverings painted and placed on the bride, like she were going to the costume party of her life, a great masquerade ball where the true woman must be hidden from sight lest the groom see her as she is and as she will be and be struck by a change of heart or a change of desire and run for the hills before his vows were publicly recorded.

"Are you all right, dear?" asked Betty Lou as she applied a thick blob of gel to a tightly pulled finger wave.

"I'm just tired," said Lily.

"She's had a lot of work to do, getting the house ready," Honey explained.

"There's nothing men love more than a done-up house," said Betty Lou. "Except maybe a done-up wife. Isn't that right, Mrs. Davis?"

"As right as grits are groceries," said Honey.

Oh, how they loved Honey Davis at

Betty's Salon. No matter how tough times might be, she was a steadfast customer. Her impeccable pageboy bob was a staple of Betty Lou's business. In fact, Honey looked so smart and unwavering as she made her way from social function to market to the country club, many of Toccoa's ladies wore their hair in similar fashion. At times, it even seemed as if Toccoa was in a bit of a bubble, defined by Honey Davis. And of course Betty Lou was only too happy to have the business of those who sought such fashion, those who came to her requesting in a whisper, "The Honey Cut." Though when a couple of Lily's friends started wearing the Honey, such things no longer struck Lily as amusing.

Lily just listened as the ladies continued their chattering.

"I understand First Baptist let Reverend White go."

"Really? That's a scandal. Why?"

"Sweetheart, when it came to actually *living* by the Good Book, Reverend White was a buffet minister."

"What do you mean?"

"Let's just say he took what he liked and left what he didn't."

Lily rolled her eyes as the women delighted in this gossip.

"That Mark Morgan sure has quieted down."

"Poor thing."

"Now I'm not sittin' on their bedpost, mind you, but I think they'd be much better off with him working for her father."

"Well, of course. It's not like he'd exactly have much working to do."

"I can't believe she'd move across the country with him."

"Harriet Horton's son brought a young woman *and* her little boy with him from Europe, halfway across the world."

"Yes, well, Harriet Horton's son got a good job with Tabor Motor Company. Have you seen Mark Morgan since he's been back? He's a simple soul, bless his heart."

"Simple" was a polite way of saying "slow," or "not right in the head." Honey could see these comments were not sitting well with her daughter.

"How are the plans coming for Nora Belle's showers, Barbara?" said Honey, changing the topic, deftly maneuvering the woman as she was so skilled at doing.

"Fabulously," Barbara Johns, a fellow

Toccoa Country Club member, responded. "Which reminds me. We've scheduled a trousseau party on March 21 and the bride-elect simply loves white phalaenopsis. I know it's a long shot and I hope you don't mind my asking, but where *did* you get all those beautiful orchids for Lily's shower?"

"I don't mind you asking at all. We're flattered that you liked them. Aren't we, Lily?"

"Yes, ma'am. I am so glad that you liked them."

"Walter had them imported from Guatemala."

"Well, of course, I should have suspected. I don't think we'll be able to arrange such an exotic venture."

"We have the most beautiful Cherokee roses at Holly Hills," said Lily. "And they'll be in peak bloom when you'd want them."

Silence. A few of the ladies fidgeted nervously in their salon chairs.

"Well, bless your heart, Lily. That is so sweet and I simply adore Cherokee roses. But I'm not sure a wildflower is quite appropriate. Nora Belle's only going to get married once, and so I think she deserves to have an event of singular splendor. Something almost as nice as yours, dear."

"Thank you, Barbara," said Honey.

"If we can't get orchids, white snapdragons, perhaps. Cherokee roses strike me as something for a *common* wedding. Know what I mean, dear?"

"I know exactly what you mean," said Lily in a decidedly pointed way that left Mrs. Johns feeling uneasy. "Good afternoon." Lily stood up and walked out.

"I'll talk to Walter, Barbara. I suspect the company would love to use its resources to make your daughter's trousseau party unforgettable," said Honey, scrambling to follow the impetuous wake of her restless daughter.

Honey caught up to Lily on the sidewalk on Doyle Street.

"That was rude."

"Mrs. Johns is worse than rude," Lily said, whipping around to face Honey.

"Yes, but that's not the point, Lily. You live here. This is your community and the Johnses are part of it. When my father's appendix burst, Barbara Johns' father removed it. And he came to our house every day for a month to check on him."

"Mother, did you always plan to spend your whole life here?"

"What kind of question is that?" she asked sternly.

"Did you ever dream of leaving Toccoa?" Lily sighed, unable to contain her exasperation.

"What has gotten into you today, Lily?"

Honey looked long and hard at her daughter.

"When your father asked me to marry him, it was the happiest day of my life. But the day before the wedding, I was feeling . . . well, I think how you're feeling right now."

"And how's that?"

"The night before the wedding your father and I got into a huge fight. He'd been drinking and my mother had my head spinning with all manner of details regarding seating arrangements and he said I didn't pay him enough attention at the rehearsal dinner and, well, things just escalated until finally I threw the ring at him and said I wouldn't marry him if he was the last living male in Dixie." Honey laughed to herself, taken away by the recollection. "In the middle of the night, my father went to the Traveler's Rest and got your father out of bed and made it clear in no uncertain terms that he was standing next to me at the altar in the morning come hell or high water. The ceremony was a little late—it took half the bridal party to find that ring—but things worked out, as they always do around here."

Honey grabbed her daughter's shoulders as if to steady her.

"You had two weeks, Lily. That's not a marriage. That's a fling is what it is."

Lily took that in, wondering if that's what Honey would call her time with Jake, wondering if that's what *she* should call it.

"For all practical purposes, your marriage starts tomorrow," Honey said, sounding supportive, even motherly. "It's perfectly natural to be a little nervous. But listen to me. He's a good boy, Paul. He's a good young man. And you are going to be happy with him. Of course you are going to be so happy with him."

"You didn't answer my question."

"Did I ever dream of leaving Toccoa?

No. No, I did not. This is my home, and my place. I dreamed of your father, and of you. And Jonathan."

Lily watched her mother's eyes fluttering, fighting tears. Honey looked away. This was the first time since the day they received the news, two and a half years ago, that Lily had heard her mother mention her brother by name.

After a brief moment, Honey straightened and smiled, reapplying her public composure as though it were fresh lipstick. "You really should powder your nose before coming downtown in summer, Lily. You're glistening."

Honey waved a happy greeting to a friend and headed toward Keener's Market.

Lily wiped perspiration off her nose. Southern women didn't sweat, of course. They glistened. Like peaches in the dew. Especially in downtown Toccoa in July.

Lily followed her mother, now in her wake of perfect composure.

The small brass bell over the door rang as Lily and Honey entered Keener's Market. It had been ringing so much today, thoughts of Christmas came to the minds of many who shopped there. Indeed, a festive atmosphere filled the general store.

"Don't you look pretty, Lily," said Evelyn Tabor. Her daughter, Mary, stood by her side holding a small American flag on a stick.

"Thank you, Mrs. Tabor."

"Did Marvin get the Cadillac contract?" asked Honey.

"He's still working on it. But it looks very promising."

While Honey and Evelyn discussed how exciting it would be for Toccoa to have its own Cadillac distributorship, Lily watched the dark-haired boy working for Mrs. Keener. Lily saw Mary exchange a smile with the boy, who couldn't have been more than a few years older than the little girl.

Lost in the moment, Lily didn't notice the man approaching the counter where Mrs. Keener and the boy were working.

"Afternoon, ma'am," he said.

"Good afternoon."

"Might you have any rice in the store?" the man asked politely.

Lily recognized the voice. Her heart quickened, surging something through her blood that made her feel that she should run—either to the man or out the door.

"Sure, we got rice."

Mrs. Keener turned to the boy. "Vincent, get me a box of rice please. White box. Over there." Mrs. Keener pointed to a row of Uncle Ben's white rice.

The boy grabbed a box and swiftly brought it to Mrs. Keener. "Thank you, Vincent."

"Yes, ma'am," the boy said shyly, a thick Sicilian accent notable in his speech.

Mrs. Keener handed the box to the man and moved on. He turned to the boy and, now with him facing her, Lily could see that it was Jake. She watched from her distance as Jake spoke to the boy in Italian.

"*Salve. Di dove sei?*" asked Jake.

"*Di Catania,*" Vincent said.

"**Sul mare. Scommetto che nuoti bene.**"

"**Si.**"

"**Che ci fai qui?**"

"**Mia madre ha sposato il Luogotentente Horton.**"

"**Ho capito. Mica sai dove potrei trovare del risotto da queste parti?**"

"*Da queste parti?*" The boy laughed.

"Mi sa che per trovarlo deve arrivare fino a Milano, signore."

Jake laughed, too.

Mrs. Keener marched over to Jake.

"Hey. Hey, what are you doing?"

"I was just—"

"Don't talk to him like that."

"I'm sorry."

"Vincent, there's a crate of watermelons in the back. Please unload them."

"Yes, ma'am," said the boy as he scurried off.

"We don't speak the enemy's language here, mister."

"I'm sorry." Jake placed the box of rice on the counter next to the register.

"That be all." It was really more of a statement than a question.

Jake just nodded. As Mrs. Keener began to ring him up, he watched the boy disappear into the back of the store. Jake felt a surge of sadness and frustration rising in his throat, but he knew enough not to put words to these emotions and just stared silently at this place around him, this town, this world.

Having overheard the exchange, Honey and Evelyn were watching now.

"The pyrotechnics man," Evelyn whispered.

"Handsome." Honey took him in.

"Lily, are you okay?" asked Evelyn. "You look a bit peaked."

"It's so hot in here. I'll wait for you outside, Mother."

Before Honey could say anything, Lily headed for the door, the brass bell jangling as she quickly walked out into the humid air.

On the sidewalk, Lily caught her breath. She looked over her shoulder and saw him through the shop windows, standing there at the counter, in his work shirt and jeans, buying his boxed item like any other person in Toccoa, but of course he was nothing like anyone else. He was a man from another place, a man from another land, with another language—hands that were now holding a box of rice were just hours ago holding her—and any moment now he was going to walk out that door and bump right into her, and one way or another that would be the end of her. She scanned the sidewalk across the street and saw Mark in his wheelchair. She crossed Doyle and went to him.

Mark was parked in the shade of a live oak tree on the sidewalk in front of a storefront with DR. DELBERT REED GENERAL PRACTITIONER lettered on frosted glass windows. Dr. Reed, Barbara Johns' father, provided a variety of medical services, ranging from setting broken bones to obstetrical care. Mark had a small, sharp pair of scissors in his hands and was lazily cutting a sheet of thick black paper. Lily stood beside him.

"Nice hair." Mark smirked without looking up.

"Stop it."

"It's nice to see you, Lily."

Lily stared silently across the street at Keener's.

"I've thought about you," he said.

"Everyone was surprised that you and Jenna moved west," she said with affection.

"Amazing how simple and small the world seemed not so long ago," he said.

"Why didn't you come home, Mark?"

"Why'd you marry the tall, blond Coca-Cola guy?"

"You know why."

"Yes. Because he fit."

"I think you and Jenna fit."

"I've known you since you were ten years old, Lily Davis. You can't lie to me. Jenna's a rich girl who fell in love with a bad boy in uniform. Didn't you hear? I married Jenna for her family's money," he said bitterly.

"Did you?"

"Maybe. Probably. I don't know. I *was* a bad boy, some stupid kid who didn't know what he wanted to make of his life. Didn't think about it. Didn't care about anything. Except one thing."

"And what was that?"

"Boy, you're clueless."

"What are you talking about?"

"Don't you know why I didn't come home?"

"To get away from Toccoa," Lily assumed.

"Yeah. And to get away from you."

As Lily absorbed this, Jake walked out of Keener's Market, down the sidewalk, and headed toward his truck.

"Trousseaus and wedding gowns, spring flowers and bridal showers. It's all so meaningless. I knew I'd never be anything to you. And I was fine with that. Everyone, everything, it was a lark to you. Your life was like a stone perpetually skipping across the lake, never dipping into it. But when you married that guy just because he fit the town's definition of what Lily Davis' husband was supposed to be, it tore me up inside."

Shifting uncomfortably in the heat on the sidewalk, Lily felt herself being torn up inside, listening to Mark, watching Jake. "Mark, I had no idea," she said, eyes downcast.

"Yes, you did. You just didn't want to."

She knew that he was right and she began to hate herself for it, for being so carefree about someone's affections, so frivolous with someone's feelings. Listening to him, she could see now that she really was like that. "Mark—"

"It's okay now. Listen, Jenna might be a silly girl, but she has the courage to follow her heart. When I was lying in that field outside Le Havre, I promised myself that if I survived, I'd take Jenna and make a life for us, some place where we weren't subject to the strings of her family's money, and the definitions of Toccoa, Georgia. Well, I got that second chance and I plan to live my life with no regrets. Whatever you do with *your* life, Lily, I truly hope that you can say the same."

Down the street, Jake opened the door to his truck. Listening to Mark, watching Jake, the sights and sounds and smells of downtown Toccoa, Lily felt like a little girl spinning on the lawn at Holly Hills, arms out, the world whizzing by, losing her balance, about to fall. But there was no joy to this, just the escalating sense that everything was spinning out of control.

As she watched Jake, Mark put something in her hands, the black cardboard silhouette, on top of white paper, that he had been cutting. It was a cutout of a girl looking up into a moon-filled sky while holding someone's hand. The image was cut off before it was clear whose hand she was holding.

Lily took in the picture.

She looked up and watched as Jake drove by.

She looked hard at Mark, realizing just how clueless she truly had been and perhaps truly was. After a moment, Jenna walked out of the doctor's office and kissed Mark on the head just as Honey appeared with a large shopping bag in her arms.

"Well, there you are," said Honey. "Are you coming?"

As Lily thought long and hard about that question, the silhouette of the solitary girl dangling in her hand, Jenna smiled and began to sing, slowly, almost hauntingly.

"'You smile, and the angels sing. And though it's just a gentle murmur at the start. We kiss, and the angels sing. And leave their music ringing in my heart.'"

"Lily, are you coming?" asked Honey.

Swept up by the proximity of such sweetness and sorrow, Lily just stood there in the thick air.

"Lily?"

THE GATHERING STORM

In the afternoon, storm clouds, the western edge of a growing tropical storm that had blown in from the Atlantic, typical for this time of year, gathered rapidly over northern Georgia. Preoccupied with things more important to her than the weather, Lily did not notice.

She stood in the sprawling white-tiled kitchen at Holly Hills wearing a fine robin's egg blue dress and a pearl necklace and helped her mother roast a goose. Honey loved entertaining and she was pulling out all the stops for Lily's in-laws, the Woodwards. As always at Honey's events, everything had to be perfect, including Lily.

Between stuffing and basting and incessant seasoning, Honey talked excitedly and relentlessly. GiGi, who had worked for the Davises for over three decades, stood nearby removing plates from their protective coverings. Unlike Honey, she noted Lily's lack of enthusiasm.

"Your father and I really want to give you and Paul a proper honeymoon," said Honey.

"Mother, that's really not necessary."

"Now I've given this a great deal of thought and I've looked into The Peabody in Memphis, though I understand they still allow those insufferable ducks in the lobby, which is a tradition I for one can live without, and I was leaning toward the Biltmore in Coral Gables, which of course is gorgeous, but apparently they're still using it as a hospital. Oh, can you just imagine! The good fortune of those poor boys, convalescing on those plush red carpets, under the palms in the Florida sun!"

Lily pulled the remaining entrails out of the goose and tossed them into a steel bowl. Accustomed to her mother's monologues, she did not respond.

"Now there *is* the Cloister at Sea Island," Honey continued, crumbling some bread for the stuffing. "And I understand the Coffin family has done a simply marvelous job of retiling that fabled pool, and you know Paul will simply adore the beach, don't you think?"

Lily just shoved a handful of bread crumbs into the goose's innards. The smell of the bird's internal organs mixed with the scent of Honey's Evening in Paris was dizzying.

"I know, I know, what about the links?" Honey said, plucking a few tiny overlooked feathers from the goose's wings. "Well, I've toyed with the idea of Augusta, but I think he'd rather have his wife in a bathing suit! What young man wouldn't, right? So the Cloister it is. Unless, well . . ."

Lily and GiGi exchanged a look as Honey lost herself in the fantasy of honeymoon possibility.

"There *is* the Waldorf-Astoria," Honey said.

"Yes, Mother, there's always the Waldorf," said Lily, who had heard all about her mother's Big Apple shopping trips.

"Imagine—Waldorf salads in the Starlight

Roof, holding hands over Park Avenue, dancing under the stars." Honey actually started to do a few steps of a waltz as though she could hear the orchestra playing in the Waldorf's Starlight Roof, which Lily had heard, as it was so often broadcast on the radio.

Suddenly, Honey froze with a thought. "Oh, Lily!"

"Yes, Mother, what is it?"

"The Breakers! Palm Beach. Your father is attending a conference down there Labor Day weekend. We could meet you and Paul. Now *that* is an idea. Oh, and about that bathing suit which you most certainly would need, let me show you some ideas I have for you."

Honey produced a page that she had torn from a recent *Redbook* magazine featuring "scandalously marvelous" two-piece bathing suits from France, the latest style, which allowed a section of midriff below the breast to be exposed. Honey wanted to order one for Lily, in yellow, with a matching frilled swim cap, and nothing Lily could say would change Honey's mind, so Lily found herself agreeing to the gift. GiGi shared a conspiratorial look with Lily about all this.

Lily's in-laws, the Woodwards, arrived at 4:30 and cocktails were served soon thereafter in the living room. Peter Woodward was a large man who spent much of his time on the golf course and the rest of it serving on a diverse assortment of corporate and philanthropic boards. Beth-Anne Smithgall Woodward was an unobtrusive southern lady whose family's long-held real estate wealth enabled her husband's predilections for the greens. Both possessing remarkably rich southern drawls, words loitered on their tongues like drunken drifters when they spoke, and Lily found herself leaning forward impatiently, awaiting and seeking a point in their wandering and melodious speech. At times, they made Lily crazy, but they were good people and they absolutely adored her.

Between wickedly dry Tanqueray martinis and the requisite warm buttered saltines—a traditional staple of the most prestigious southern country clubs, soda crackers literally soaked in clarified butter and then toasted—Lily sat quietly while the Woodwards and the Davises engaged in loud and generally self-congratulatory conversation that seemed to go on interminably. There was a great deal of extremely animated discussion regarding the new models of automobiles that the manufacturers would soon once again make available to the consumer market. Mr. Woodward remarked repeatedly about the great sacrifice this country had made by forgoing new models since 1942 while the manufacturers in Detroit contributed their resources and production might solely to the successful prosecution of the war. With the fighting now finally terminating in Europe and soon to be ending in the Pacific, 1945 promised to be a very exciting year for new car models. While Mr. Davis and Mr. Woodward discussed which model of Cadillac they felt Paul would like most from the company, Mrs. Woodward shared her wishes to take Paul to the Buckhead Men's Shop soon after his arrival, since he would most certainly need an entire new wardrobe, as styles had changed significantly since he left. Mrs. Woodward, who seemed to have much of her son's schedule for the next week or so preplanned, including a lunch at the Piedmont Driving Club—the PDC, as she called it—had already set up an appointment for him with a tailor whom she seemed to know a great deal about. Lily participated as much as she could, offering her thoughts on Paul's tastes in fashion, a subject she realized she knew virtually nothing about.

Mainly, Lily looked out the window and watched heavy drops of rain pummeling the scorched magnolia leaves.

The conversation, now lubricated by copious amounts of fine gin, carried over into the dining room and continued throughout the highly fashionable Green Goddess salad with anchovy fillets, the cucumber soup, the low country–style crab cake, and Honey's famous roast stuffed goose, which she explained once again was an Alsatian dish and not a German one. Lily talked politely, sipping at cold and notably unremarkable rosé in a huge crystal balloon glass. Watching the others at the table, drinking from the Waterford and eating off the Wedgwood with the Reed & Barton, she felt as though she was getting a glimpse of what the rest of her life might very well look and sound and smell like. Clinking bone china, the ghastly aftertaste of silver polish on corpulent hunks of rare goose, thin red fluid sloshing around in oversized goblets, it all made her think about death, and the discussion about the great wealth that Henry Coffin had left the remaining Coffin family members who inherited the Cloister, where it was decided that Lily should in fact honeymoon, put her over.

She felt a chill up her spine, and then she began to hyperventilate. She'd always been wired for these kinds of odd feelings, like how she felt in Auraria, but somehow the last few days had connected her to something that kept sending these currents through her, and this one amidst all this dreadful imagery made her feel that something terrible was going to happen and she became convinced that if she didn't get out of here immediately she would pass out.

Lily stood, a sort of panic in her eyes. She had to get to Jake. She had to get to him now.

By the time the fresh peach cobbler with

basil garnish was served on the antique Royal Worcester dessert plates accompanied by the dessert forks and extra-long sterling teaspoons with the matching coffee service for the Stewarts, no one noticed that Lily had excused herself to get home before the roads got bad from the storm.

No one except Walter.

It was dark when Lily pulled out of Holly Hills and onto Highway 123. Rain pounded on the Packard, reverberating through the car and into her bones. The wipers going full speed, banging on the steel frame of the windshield like a metronome out of control, she still could not see more than a few feet in front of her. Feeling the banging of the wipers in her teeth, she gripped the rigid wheel so tight, sweat from her palms began to drip down her wrists.

Boom! A thunderclap shook the car and Lily jumped in the seat.

Catching her breath, she wiped perspiration from her forehead and cursed herself. She'd been in a daze, since leaving Jake and then seeing her father, all afternoon, into the evening, a daze. *How could*

I have let it get so late? She told Jake she'd meet him in the afternoon and somehow the hours got away from her and she had to see him. She had to snap out of this. She *had* to see him.

Despite the thick, dark sheets of rain, Lily sped up. The pounding increased, the banging got louder. Water along the road shot through the grooves of the wide rubber tires as they raced along ever faster.

Leaning forward over the wheel, Lily tried to see through the hazy windshield out into the rain and darkness. Headlights reflecting off the fog, she squinted, trying to make sure there was nothing ahead of her in the road, her foot pushing even further on the accelerator, engine pistons firing harder, tires turning even faster in the building water along the road. Her insides jumped as she thought she saw a deer in the road, but it was just the fog, and she pushed even further on the gas.

Her head jolting to the right, she saw the sign for Owl Swamp Road, the turn she needed to make, flying by in the streaming rain.

"Damn it!"

Lily hit the brakes hard, and they locked

up, the tires hitting more water than they could disperse and the Packard losing traction with the road. Frantically Lily turned the steering wheel and jammed the brakes, but there was no response as the tires slid along a slick layer of rainwater covering the surface of the asphalt like a bowling ball flying down a waxed lane, like an unsteered sled on a sheet of ice, until the car flew off the road and onto the shoulder and hit the thick, soaking clayous dirt and skidded and splashed to a muddy stop just inches in front of a massive oak tree.

Tilted sideways in the mud on the side of the road, the Packard's red brake lights shone bright through the murky rain.

Inside the car, Lily stared at the tree right in front of her as bucketfuls of wet Georgia red clay, the color of blood, just sprayed up from her car, dripped slowly down the trunk.

Rain still pounding, wipers still beating, Lily took a deep breath and tried to compose herself, but the mud running down the tree seemed to point out to her just how serious the state of her life had become.

Sitting in that car on the side of the road in her robin's egg blue dress and her pearls, the rain falling all around her, Lily felt like nature was trying to keep her from Jake. For her own good? She didn't know. Were forces conspiring to keep her in her place? She didn't know. But among the haze of questions, strangely, she could feel a clarity rising. If nothing else, a child-like determination, manifest in adult woman form.

For if she was in fact destined to be some eighty-year-old lady sitting on her porch with nothing in her life on which to reflect and savor but Tanqueray and tonics and buttered saltines and silver and china and goose, that stinking bloody goose, and a heart kept comfortable but never heated or stirred or truly known, she would surely go mad, but one more time . . . if she could have just one more time to touch Jake Russo again, to feel the warmth of his face, the embrace of his arms, to look into his eyes just one more time . . . that might be enough. Could she give him up after that? She did not know. But she was sure be-yond all boundaries of doubt that if she did not have one more time with him she might as well hit the accelerator right now and put this vehicle and herself into that oak tree, because she truly felt that from this moment on her life would be unlivable if she could not see Jake Russo one more time. And it was going to take a hell of a lot more than rain to keep her from him.

Lily hit the gas again and the Packard's rear wheels spun in the mud. She could not believe this. She was not going to be stuck here by the side of the road. No way! Steeling her grip on the hard ridges of the wheel, she hit the gas again hard, dangerously so. The tires threw mud into the black sky, but the car didn't move.

Lily didn't care if this was nature trying to stop her or test her, or kill her, she didn't care about anything except seeing him again, and a determination, even a recklessness that she had never before known she was capable of, raged through her and she shook the wheel, turning it back and forth, her foot pumping the gas, and finally the Packard lurched out of the red mud and onto the road and she whipped the wheel around, quickly turning the Packard, and headed back in the direction she had just come.

Her mind and body as alert and focused as they were designed to ever be in a time of crisis, Lily saw the road she had missed, slowed the vehicle, and made the turn, and then she pressed hard on the gas again, increasing her speed as she drove anxiously through the fog, her heart pounding, her mind running, as she prayed that he was still there, prayed from a place in the core of her core, please, please, let him know she was coming, let him know she would be there, please, let him wait, oh, please—*let him wait*. Racing in the pouring rain down Owl Swamp Road, Lily pleaded with all that she was and all that she would ever be that she be given one more chance to see and touch and hold and kiss Jake Russo.

She threw open the door of the cabin and just stood there, breathless, completely drenched and covered in wet mud, illuminated by a crack of lightning behind her.

After a moment, Jake walked over to her.

He had waited. All afternoon, into the evening, of course he had waited.

A WALK IN THE RAIN

They tore at each other's clothing, and before they were even fully undressed they began to make love, hard and fast and furious. No moderation, no deliberation. Their enmeshed bodies both now wet. Their cries immediate and full and unending, of both what they were doing to each other and all that was pent up leading to this. It was as though a match had been lit inside the fireworks truck and everything exploded all at once. He bit his lip. Her necklace broke and pearls spilled and scattered all over the wood and dirt floor.

Neither had ever had a need so complete, to be entirely with the other. A confluence of drives had come together and both knew that this bond, hearts pounding, flesh contracting and releasing, the building cadence and culmination of it all, joined them not only to each other but also to something beyond themselves, and now, no matter what and in no matter what way, this connection would always be.

Whatever questions may have remained since last they were together were now answered.

Afterward, they lay on the blankets in the flush of a fire that Jake had made in the stone hearth. Rain continued to fall, its thumping patter made soft and mellifluous by the kudzu.

As reflexively as he breathed, Jake stroked her soaking wet hair. Lily reached out to his face, touching his mouth tenderly.

"You're bleeding," she said.

Lily wiped blood from his lips. She saw that his eyelids had fallen and she realized that he was asleep.

Lily smiled, partially out of relief. For this was the first time that she had ever seen Jake Russo sleep. This was the first time she had ever seen him at any kind of rest. She kissed him on the head, and that was when she realized that she loved him.

Tullahoma, Tennessee, January 30, 1942

The young soldier stood near the thick-gauge chain-link fence as inconspicuously as he could. It was very high and topped with rolled razor wire. Five feet inside was a second identical fence, same height, also topped with razor wire. Through the dual fences he could see dozens of men in fraying green apparel as they marched from their rows of hastily constructed ply-wood huts to a mess tent. Trenches had been dug between the huts to drain off water, but they were filled with ice. The ground throughout the encampment was covered with half-frozen mud, broken apart by jeep tracks, and the men slogged through it. Already showing obvious signs of malnourishment, the men shivered in the bitter conditions. Many blew into their raw hands, fingers exposed through torn cotton gloves, exhaling billows of moist fog.

He had tried to prepare himself for what

he saw, but he had no idea Tennessee could be so cold. He had no idea this place would be so brutal.

"Ernesto Russo. Have you seen Ernest Russo?" he said to some of the men as they slogged by.

The men looked startled, even scared, and quickly moved on. A few shook their heads.

"Ernesto Russo. Has anyone seen Ernest Russo?" He said it louder so some of the men walking farther inside could hear him. But no one responded. A couple just shot him worried looks. *Who is this young man?* He had a very short crew cut and wore an Army uniform with no insignia, denoting a new recruit who had not yet completed basic training.

"Ernesto Russo."

"Halt! You there! Halt!" a voice screamed from the guard tower. A machine gun in the tower swung around on its mount and trained on him.

Adrenaline surged through his veins. He wheeled around toward the forest. Poised to make a run for it.

"Halt right there!"

The pinewoods were just twenty, maybe thirty feet away. He could make it.

The men inside froze still and watched.

Another gun trained on him. Two more guards began yelling.

"Stop where you are!"

"Don't move, Private!"

Just as he was about to run—

"Don't shoot!" A voice called out from inside. "That's my son!"

"Papa!"

He turned and saw his father, Ernesto, cling both hands on the inside fence. He grabbed the outer fence. Separated by the sixty inches of frozen soil, they faced each other through the chain links.

"What are you doing here? Are you crazy?"

"I had to know you were okay."

"Jake. Jake. You shouldn't have come."

Before he could answer, a jeep pulled up behind Jake and two Army sergeants jumped out and grabbed him.

"Get your hands off me!" Jake started to shake them off, but the armed soldiers made it immediately clear who was in charge here.

"Please, give us a minute," Ernesto pleaded. "That's my son. Please. Just one minute."

"That your father, Private?" one of the guards asked.

"Yes, Sergeant."

The guard softened. He looked Jake up and down, evaluating the situation. He saw RUSSO lettered on Jake's plain Army uniform and immediately understood. The guard deeply respected the importance of his duty. But this was a part of it that he hated. The gray area. There were very few questions in this war. Good and evil were clearly identifiable. Usually. The sergeant had found, or at least had begun to sense, that those parameters didn't always apply so neatly here in his hastily constructed internment camp. Nevertheless, he told himself, the evil they faced was so grave and victory over it so vital, his duty in this gray place was necessary.

"One minute," he said.

Both sergeants stepped back and lit cigarettes. The running jeep engine spewed exhaust into the frigid South Tennessee air.

"Look at you." Ernesto took in his son's uniform and buzz cut.

"They recruited me just a few weeks after they grabbed you."

"You look good." The older man's sallow eyes beamed with pride. "But you shouldn't have come, Giacobbe. How did you find me?"

"Congressman Bowers spoke to the FBI and told Mother. I got a letter from her last week at Fort McClellan, in Alabama, where I'm doing basic. We got a leave before they ship us off next week."

"And this is where you came?"

"Why are you here?"

"Jake . . ."

"How can I fight? Who am I fighting for? *What* am I fighting for?"

"So many questions."

"Who am I?"

"You are Giacobbe Antonio Russo. Son of Ernesto, nephew of Federico. You are my flesh, the blood of Italia, and you are an American. Do you understand me?"

"Mother said the FBI wouldn't explain why you were here."

"When your uncle came over after fighting in the First World War, every month I sent five percent of the family's earnings to the Associazione Nazionale

Famiglie dei Caduti in Guerra. To help families of Italian veterans who suffered from the war. But not all the money goes to the families. Some of it ends up in government hands."

"You can't help that. And you *hate* the fascists."

"I speak their language."

"The language of our *ally* when Uncle fought for them."

"And of our enemy this time. Son, your uncle is an ex-Combattenti, an Italian war veteran, who lives in my house. Our money has helped Mussolini. And I have exchanged formulas for high explosives with Italian nationals."

"Fireworks! That is why you're here?"

"I am here because of fear—which is exactly what is driving those black boots across Europe. Fear is not rational. Fear does not differentiate between the ideologies of those who speak a common language. Yes, I hate fascism, and it can only thrive when there is fear. That is why you must fight. Listen to me, my son. America is a lumbering adolescent. But one day, if given a chance, this country will grow up, and you will be part of it. Fight for it. Fight for that chance. But do not let what you see, what your uncle saw, blacken your heart. War can get into a man's mind and blood and never leave, like a delirium. Listen to me. War is a dark fever, love its tonic."

The guards tossed their cigarettes to the ground and approached Jake. "Okay, let's go."

Ernesto pressed his face to the fence, gripping it. "Promise me that you will always leave your heart open."

The guards took Jake by the arms.

"Promise me!"

Dachau, Germany, April 29, 1945

The smell from the furnaces lingered. It ruminated through the woods well beyond the razor-wire-topped fences that surrounded the muddy camp like a nightmare that remains upon waking. Indeed, it was a smell that would haunt him for the rest of his life. Sulfurous and singed, coppery sweet, the remains of deer after a wildfire. It was nauseating, the stench of madness.

Hair long, uniform tattered and blood-stained, years of war behind him, Jake still had no reference point for the things he encountered in this place.

With their former prisoners sitting and lying nearby, coughing and shivering in striped rags, too weak to care about attempts at rapid justice, the two guards were dragged out by their hair. They begged for their lives in German and broken English.

Smith & Wessons out, waving wildly, pointed at them as they screamed for mercy.

"Sprechen sie Deutsch?"

"Shut up, you murderer!"

"*Sprechen sie . . .* Coca-Cola! Coca-Cola!"

"Shut up!"

"*Bitte! Bitte!* Don't kill me!"

"Murderer!"

Sidearms aimed at their heads as they writhed on the ground squealing in terror. *Pop! Pop!*

Jake took it all in, emotionless, dead to the world.

"War is a dark fever, love its tonic." Ernesto Russo stared out at Jake from behind the fence. "Promise me that you will always leave your heart open. Promise me!"

Toccoa

"Jake," Lily said softly.

Jake opened his eyes and looked into hers.

"I love you, Lily. I've seen enough and done enough to know what is true, and nothing has ever been truer. I love you."

"I love you, too. I feel like all my life I've been waiting to love you."

"Come away with me."

"Jake. Don't." She kissed him on his lips to silence him before he went any further.

He pulled away, refusing to be silenced. "I'm serious, Lily."

"I have a duty here."

"Come away with me."

She meant to say no and end it there, but another word came out. "Where?" she found herself saying.

"Nantucket. Boulder. Chicago. Soon after, Latin America. Brazil. They love fireworks in Rio. My family will send the shells down there on a containership and we'll shoot magnificent shows over Copacabana Beach at night and we'll lie in bed in our little flat nearby till noon. We'll eat in the cafés off Visconde de Pirajá in Ipanema and you can spend the afternoons working on your mosaics. After that, we'll go west to Lima and shoot over the great waves at Huanchaco Beach, and then catch a ship north, through Baja, maybe Cabo, then we'll shoot the skies across the Southwest, La Jolla, Taos, then maybe on to New York and Paris. Definitely, we'll get a show in Paris."

"Do you pray, Jake?"

"I used to."

"Why'd you stop?"

"It stopped working."

"So you think it did work once?"

"I don't know."

Lily closed her eyes for a moment. Jake just watched her, wondering if she was thinking or praying.

"Do you ever wish you could divide yourself in two?" she asked. "One life could follow all the wishes of your heart. The other life could fulfill your duties."

"You *are* living two lives, Lily. One is in a

big beautiful house in town. The other is in a kudzu-covered cabin. You've been living this way your whole life, but I don't think you can keep doing it. I think you're finally at a fork in the path and you can't go both ways and if you try to divide yourself, sooner or later you will fall apart."

"I know. I know." A lump growing in her throat, Lily remembered her father's words.

Jake put his hands on her face. "Part of you is Lily Davis and part of you is the ghost of Lily Davis, escaped from the shell that once contained her. Part of you is that Nunnehi, Lily, one of the Cherokee's invisible people, that part of you that lives here in the woods."

She turned away for a moment. He could see this was really getting to her, but he had to say it.

"Don't you see," he said, gently but firmly. "My darling, Lily, you are Princess Toccoa."

Lily nodded, fighting tears, this truth sweeping over her.

Jake looked at her hard, continuing. "Before you walk out of this forest you have to make a choice about how you want to live the rest of your life. I want you to live it with me. I want to take care of you. But it has to be *your* choice. I won't say anything else about it."

"I wish we could just lie here and listen to the rain and hold each other like this forever. Can you make this night last forever, my dear Jake? Can you use your magic to do that for me?"

"I can make it last for a few more hours."

They lay together like that well into the night, holding each other in the firelight, safe and warm, while the storm outside screamed like a banshee in the wood and rattled the world.

After scrambling to gather as many of the pearls from the broken necklace as they could find, they left the cabin in a rush before dawn. Fed by the intense heat that had warmed the waters more than usual all along the eastern seaboard, the fast-moving storm had been quite severe. Unexpectedly so. It grew suddenly in intensity and size through the night, downing trees and causing power outages as it quickly made its way north. Several pines were down in the forest. Large broken branches lay across the path. The creek had overflowed its banks, so much so that the floor of the cabin had actually been quite muddy near the walls. A few of the pearls had disappeared in the soft, wet clay.

But in the morning, the brunt of the storm had moved on, the creek receded, and a light drizzle now fell. They walked through the dripping foggy woods, holding hands, with the heavy silence of those who had resigned themselves to a fate they cannot escape.

Retracing their path, they stepped over tree limbs and walked through muddy piles of fallen leaves. Once again, Jake held Lily's hand tight as they made their way across the creek, loud and swollen, the morning mist rising over it like a ghost. Crossing over the creek, they disappeared in the mist for a brief moment, and then reappeared as they found footing in the boggy soil on the other side.

As much as Lily wanted to stay in the forest or run off with Jake, the duty of which her father spoke became clearer in her mind with the rising sun. She was leaving the wood and its fantasies, not unlike the many times she had run home from here as a girl, and in moments she would have to make a choice about this man beside her, this beautiful man, and that choice was becoming clear. Toccoa was her home, she told herself, and she had more than just a life here, more than what she had told him about during their dinner in the field, more than what she had told herself—she had a duty, to which she had committed herself.

Feeling the fog, bodiless and thick, on her face, Jake's hand in hers, as she walked out of the woods she closed her eyes and let his love pour into her. Could that be enough? Could she keep it close, let it feed her spirit and not pull her down when he was gone?

She thought she could. Yes, she thought she could do what she *had* to do, what she knew she had to do.

They approached the Packard parked on the side of the road. When they got there, Lily turned to Jake, grabbed both his hands, and lifted her chin as bravely as she could.

"Listen to me," she said more intensely than he had ever heard her. "I want you to find someone. Do you hear me? I want you to take that passion of yours and find someone wonderful and give it to her. Give it all to her. Do you hear me?!"

Jake just stared at her, his heart breaking. He knew she was right for going. If there was one thing he understood, it was the calling of duty. And her strength only made him love her more.

"Will you do that for me?" she pleaded.

He did not respond. He could not respond.

"Jake, listen to me." She put her hands on his face and held him tightly. "Just because the sky is already filled with stars, it doesn't mean you can't make your own."

And she kissed him, deep and quick, and she turned and got in her car. She started the engine, put it in gear, pulled onto the road, and drove off.

She watched him in the rearview mirror, standing in the rain, getting smaller and fading away, tears falling down her face. *I will never see him again*, she thought to herself, she would never see him again, and it was no longer an idea in the distance, it was real and it was happening, right before her, he was fading away and disappearing right before her eyes and so was his love and all that they had shared and ever could have shared, it was getting smaller and she could feel it going and it was breaking her into tiny countless immeasurable pieces inside, and as hard as she had known it was going to be, this was worse, unfathomably worse.

He just stood there on the side of the road, oblivious to everything but her driving away. The emotionless veil falling on him again, the deadness beginning to set his heart to stone once again, and inside he fought it, telling himself not to lose what they had, not to let go what she had kindled in him.

Suddenly she stopped the car.

Red brake lights shone brightly through the mist.

She threw the door open and jumped out of the Packard. She ran toward him. He started walking toward her and then broke into a run.

They met and embraced in the middle of the road, the rain still falling around them.

"I can't give you up! I can't!" she said, sobbing.

"Then don't."

They kissed. And in an instant the entire world came alive once more.

"Take me with you," Lily said.

"Anywhere you want."

Committing herself to leaving Jake for even those few moments, watching him fade away behind her—the *reality* of it—hit Lily with the recognition that as important as her duty was to Paul Woodward, her obligation to fulfill her commitment to serve as his wife, there was an even greater calling, and Paul Woodward would survive her response to it, maybe even better with someone more suited for him, surely, even better, someone who did not carry what she carried when she looked in that rearview mirror, and that, someday, she began to believe, might heal the damage that this would do.

"I'll tell him when he comes home," she said, feeling both elated and scared but also determined. "I'll meet you in the field as soon as I can get away and I'll leave with you after the show tomorrow." She kissed him again. "Nothing is going to keep me from you. Nothing."

Lily jogged back to the Packard. Again,

Jake stood there and watched her drive off, this time until she had finally disappeared down the road.

Toccoa, July 3, 1945

Early in the morning, Lily Davis Woodward, twenty years old, her entire life before her, pulled up to her big house with the wraparound porch on the northern edge of Toccoa prepared to make her fate.

She parked the Packard, got out, slammed the door behind her, and as she began to approach that porch . . .

A cell phone rang.

PATHS

Toccoa, 2007

Captain Stokes was so captivated with eighty-two-year-old Lily's story that she didn't even notice Colleen's cell phone ringing in the Stephens County Historical Society office. Colleen finally answered it.

"I'm sorry," Colleen said into the phone. "No. I won't be there. I'll call you later. I . . . I can't explain right now. I will call you later."

Lily knew that her granddaughter was talking to her fiancé, who was none too pleased with her right now. But Colleen, for once, didn't seem to care.

Colleen stood, walked away from the table, and continued the conversation in private across the room. Clearly, her fiancé was upset that she was still here and not meeting him, but she was taking a stand. Lily just watched, the haze of emotion from her story still hanging over her as she rested her voice for a few moments.

Stokes got up and turned on some lights in the office, as it was getting late and the sunlight was fading.

After a few moments, Colleen hung up, turned off her phone, and put it away. She walked back over to the table and sat, exchanging a long silent look with Lily.

"What did you do, Grandma?" Colleen finally said, much more interested in Lily's life right now than her own.

Stokes expectantly sat back down as well.

"I walked up the steps to my house," eighty-two-year-old Lily continued, sadness now filling her eyes. "Ready to tell Paul everything. It had been three years. It would hurt him, of that I was fairly certain. But three years. I was a child when we married. I truly felt he would understand that I had changed. And after all, was it really my responsibility to stay married to Paul when I felt what I did for Jake? Was there really a duty greater than what I felt in my soul? Turns out, there was."

As twenty-year-old Lily approached her porch, Walter Davis opened the front door of Lily's house. In the light of the new day, he looked tired and weathered as he walked out onto the porch. Lily froze on her walkway for a moment when she saw him standing there. She took a deep breath and then marched up the steps with her head up. As she reached the porch and approached her father, just as she was about to start speaking, he spoke first.

"Lily, there's been an accident," Walter Davis said.

She stopped in her tracks.

As she stood there on the porch trying to process what this meant, Honey burst out of the front door, hysterical, and threw her arms around Lily.

Stokes and Colleen just gazed at the old woman who spoke to them in the office.

"There were eighteen souls on board the C-54," Lily explained evenly to them.

"All of them perished on the treeless plains of Nova Scotia. They said the plane missed its flight window and encountered an un-anticipated storm, the far northern edge of the same system that came through Toc-coa that night. The plane charted a quick course around it, but the storm was bigger and more violent than expected. It's funny how things work out. Sixty million people died during the war, half a million Ameri-cans. Paul Woodward survived all that but perished just a few hundred miles from home because his plane simply ran out of gas. You see, as it turns out, that path you choose might never take you in the direc-tion you had thought. Jake was right. We make our plans, but the difference be-tween life and death is a breath, a heart-beat, the direction we choose to go. So in the end, there actually was something that could keep me from Jake Russo. Not the responsibility of being someone else's wife. But the duty of being a widow."

Nearly every moment on that terrible day in 1945, Lily's house was filled with a con-stant stream of people. They surrounded her. She looked dazed, a reaction most fully expected, but those who got near her could see that it was deeper, trancelike, to those who got very close, frighteningly so.

She had found love, been ready to give it up, then decided to throw everything away for it no matter what, and then to be hit with this . . . this entirely unexpected act of nature . . . it was more than she ever could have imagined. If anything, what did it all mean?

On the outside, limply, she found herself going through the actions of accepting expressions of grief, while inside hair-trigger actions that had profound repercussions on not just her life but the lives of everyone she'd ever loved and known and probably ever would love or know raveled through her head like writing on biblical scrolls, and a state of shock seized her.

"All day and all evening, they came and went, as they had in so many houses in so many American towns. This was an especially all too common scene in Toccoa during those years. And the town was prepared to turn out comfort at a moment's notice. They came from all over North Georgia. The Piedmont Driving Club ladies. The Commerce Club gentlemen. The mayor of Gainesville came to my house and held my hand. Many of the company folk even came up from Atlanta. I hear that Robert W. Woodruff himself paid a call late in the day, but I did not see him. It didn't matter that Paul's plane did not go down in combat, it didn't matter that technically he was not under arms for the military. We were given the same respect and gratitude and condolences as any other beloved members of the community who had lost someone making the greatest sacrifice for his country and his family."

That night, her house bustling with friends and neighbors, business leaders and area dignitaries, Lily stood alone on her porch and looked out over the dark sky. It seemed even darker than usual.

She thought about disappearing into the night. She thought about running off. But before she acted on those thoughts, her father came out and joined her. He put his arm around her and stood by her, silently.

Honey stepped out on the porch, visibly moved by the image of her husband and daughter standing together. She stood near them and, again, broke down with grief. Honey was inconsolable, but Walter tried to soothe her as best he could. Facing Lily, he wrapped his arms around Honey, who cried on Walter's shoulder. Lily just watched her mother grieve openly, which only drove Lily's pain deeper and further into her. More than anyone, Walter saw Lily's internal anguish. More than anyone, he understood it precisely.

While stroking the back of his wife's head, Walter Davis looked intently at his daughter. "Time. Give it time," he said.

Comforted, Honey nodded into her husband's shoulder. But more than words of comfort, more than wise counsel, it was a request, perhaps even a plea.

Lily nodded to her father, knowing that he was talking not to Honey but to *her.* Pacing the porch, considering the dark night, Lily ran it over in her mind. *Time, give it time.*

"On July 4, 1945, after spending much of a painful night with Mr. and Mrs. Woodward going through Paul's things, with an ever-increasing stream of people again pouring into my house with flowers and casseroles of every imaginable variety, the funeral arrangements were quickly set and finalized. Paul's mother's father had been an Army officer who served and died honorably in the First World War and was granted burial rights at Arlington. With a little help from the company, those rights were also granted to Paul. But we all had to leave for Washington immediately. So late in the day on the Fourth we went to the train depot. Platform Five, it was."

With Colleen and Stokes leaning forward, enthralled, Lily pointed out the glass window of the office. "That one, right over there."

"Didn't you think about going to Jake? Or sending him a note?" Colleen was incredulous.

"You have to understand. To leave my husband was one thing. It would hurt Paul and embarrass my mother and anger my father. It would be a scandal, but, eventually, they would all get over it. People would come to understand that I married when I was a child and I met my true love years later and they would eventually forgive. But to leave my deceased husband was something very different. To run off with a man I'd just met, leaving my family and community instead of attending my husband's funeral and grieving with his parents and my parents and being a dutiful widow . . . it would destroy everyone I ever cared about. It would forever tarnish Paul Woodward's memory. My actions at his death would be the defining event of his life. I couldn't do that to him. Partly because I felt responsible.

"Everyone I had ever known and ever heard about was grasping my hand and I couldn't help but wonder at the strangeness of it all, I couldn't help wondering if I had somehow caused Paul's death, because I had wished for a way out—I had prayed for it. 'Guilty' is too simple of a word to describe how I felt, but I have no other to offer. Of course I thought about going to Jake, but my father's words, his plea, kept coming back to me, kept rising above all else. Time. This was not the time to run off with someone. Time. To be a widow. Time to show respect for a husband's life. Time for duty. And for penitence. Of course I thought about writing a note. While the whole world grasped at me, and I sorted through my husband's possessions with my husband's mother and my mother, and his body was recovered and shipped and prepared and the funeral set and we were ushered off to the train, the whole time instead of grieving I composed that note in my head. *Wait for me, my darling. My duty calls, but I will return. And I will find you. Just give our love some time.* But I did not send it. How would I? How could I?"

On Independence Day, 1945, in the early evening, the Davises and the Woodwards drove to the depot together in Walter's 1942 Cadillac sedan. They drove down Highway 123 until it became Currahee Street, which took them into the center of town. They turned on Pond and then on Doyle, driving past Belk-Gallant and the Ritz and Keener's Market.

Downtown Toccoa was festooned with red, white, and blue ribbons. The remnants of the storm had been swept away and the town was celebrating. A brass band was warming up on the square in front of the courthouse. People ate hot dogs and candy apples and ice-cream cones. Children carried sparklers through the streets. Teenagers held hands. Swing poured out of the Hi-De-Ho Club, and through its big front windows Lily could see the silhouettes of couples dancing. Numbly Lily stuck her head slightly out the open window of the car and just stared, unmoved, as though watching a world in which she was no longer an inhabitant.

The Cadillac took a left on Alexander Street and parked in front of the depot. Several porters were waiting and they rushed to the car. The Director of Operations for the depot was also waiting, and he made sure that the Davises and the Woodwards and their luggage were ushered as comfortably as possible to Platform Five and onto the Washington Vestibuled Limited, which came into the depot just minutes after their arrival.

The Toccoa rail yards were always among the busiest between Charlotte and Atlanta, and tonight was certainly no exception. Iron clanged and soldering sparks lit the night as a heavy black engine was repaired in the roundhouse. A water pump screeched and coal clattered down a chute as a southbound train was readied on the tracks.

Northbound Platform Five at the Toccoa

Train Depot was teeming with people. Flag-men and conductors, firemen and porters, all scurrying to and from their trains. Soldiers in uniform arriving for the homecoming the military had scheduled. Partygoers and revelers who had come in from all around North Georgia for the celebration. A radio blasted music and a crowd of young people danced and drank bourbon and celebrated life.

Looking exhausted beyond her years, Lily, along with the Woodwards and the Davises, said good-bye to friends and boarded the train.

At nightfall, the Washington Vestibuled Limited, a deluxe liner with well-appointed all-private sleeping cars, luxurious lounge and dining cars, left the Toccoa depot heading up the Atlantic seaboard. As the Davises and Woodwards settled into their staterooms, Lily stood on a platform between cars, looked out an open door, and watched as the train pulled away.

The events of the last five days had been unlike anything she had ever encountered, had ever considered. She had no reference point to calibrate her feelings, no compass to point her. As she looked out the train door, her town beginning to move under her and away, the sum of it all left her disoriented and numb.

When the train began to gain speed, suddenly a great quaking explosion sent a shock wave through the air and a rumbling through the ground. She looked out and saw dozens of silver threads of light shooting into the sky and then exploding in a grand and splendent synchronous display of color and light and sound.

She grasped the handrails on the platform, leaned out over the tracks, peered down the car, and saw faces, scores of faces, pressed up against the window glass, looking up.

It was Jake's show, and it was magnificent, unlike anything that Lily or anyone else on that train had ever seen before.

"I thought about him alone in the shadows of the field that night, engraving the sky with his thoughts and emotions, this passionate, beautiful man, who had covered me with his body and blown on my knee and whispered to me about the secrets of his heart while he held my face and loved me. And suddenly I was alive again."

At night, in Bartam's Field, Jake lit the July 4th Toccoa Fireworks Show. Using a long "match," a three-foot wood pole aflame on one end, he danced and moved rhythmically up and down and in between the rows and rows of mortars, lighting fuses in perfect timing as he went. In the falling sparks and rising smoke, his face half lit by the glow of sulfur, Jake Russo was a man driven by the substratal forces of the elements, a man moved by the perfect symbiosis of passion and pain, of love and loss, of life and death.

"I thought about jumping off that train, and running to the source of the magic, throwing my arms around him and going with him wherever he was going. I remember thinking, *My father is wrong, and Jake is right, there is no time, there is only 'this, now,' and I am letting it slip away.*"

As the train increased its velocity, quickly pulling away from Toccoa, Lily gripped the railing with her hands and leaned over the tracks shooting by underneath her. She leaned out farther to see the fireworks exploding brilliantly in the sky above. She leaned out still farther, her hands loosening their grip on the railing.

The ground moving faster and faster below her, Lily leaned out farther.

She looked up, taking in the fireworks growing in splendor and intensity, losing herself in their magnificence and all they had come to mean to her.

Leaning out farther, the wind whipping her, she felt overwhelmed by the division within her, by the two Lilys both pulling ever harder at her, by the simultaneous beauty and sorrow of the world. What had she done? *What had she done?* What did it all mean and how did this suddenly become her life?

The fireworks exploding over her, she was that nine-and-a-half-year-old girl again, hearing the first concussive booms and running through her house, past the bergamot-scented relatives with their glowing freshly scrubbed faces and the clinking ice cubes in highball glasses and outside by the sweet-smoking kettledrum grills and her parents in their tennis whites . . . her parents, so young, so full of hope and rue and tenderness as they watched her running from them out into the expanse of lawn, the fireworks exploding over her, and he took her hand. . . .

"Something happens to people as they get older," the young man said, taking in how mesmerized young Lily was by the fireworks. "They lose what's important." Then he pointed up. "Never forget this, Lily. Never forget this."

They both looked upward, their faces cast with the dazzling colors exploding above them, and Lily could see Jonathan, her brother, so handsome, so kind, looking up with the same wonder and expansiveness and capacity for love that she felt in her own heart, a young man ready to make his own way in the world.

Lily leaned out over the tracks as the train leaving Toccoa continued to speed up, Jake's fireworks filling the sky above.

And, finally, Lily began to cry. "It was you, Jonathan. Of course, it was you. I'm so sorry. I'm so deeply, deeply sorry. I did forget. Oh, Jonathan, I miss you so much. Oh my . . . I miss you."

Just as it looked as though her hands

might slip and she might actually fall from the train—her father grabbed her, pulling her inside to safety.

Standing on the platform between cars, he held her tighter than he ever had before and she finally broke down, letting go the heavy true cries of a child in her father's arms, the deepest of cries, the fireworks over Toccoa disappearing into the distance.

Very quiet now, Lily sat at the table in the office of the Stephens County Historical Society, her weathered hands resting calmly before her, her eyes, wet, looking off into the distance as though she could still see her brother and Jake and the fireworks from those long-gone days of her life. Colleen and Stokes saw what the memories had done to her and they, too, were silent, nearly afraid to speak.

Finally, her voice cracking a bit, swallowing hard several times, Lily continued. "I left a part of me behind on the tracks that night," Lily finally said. "Something that burned and fell away. Like ashes from a firework. Like a magnolia blossom in the Toccoa sun.

"When I got back from Washington, I tried to contact him. I tried reaching him in Nantucket, but it was impossible to get a long-distance line through to the island. I was able to reach the Boulder Chamber of Commerce and they put me in touch with the motel near Folsom Field where they were accommodating him. I called the motel, and they told me to call back in eight days, when he was to arrive. I did, and was informed that a local man who had worked in munitions for the Marine Corps was meeting the truck from Lawrence County and had replaced him. I went to Atlanta and did some research and I was able to get a call through to the home of Ernesto Russo in Pennsylvania, and I spoke to Jake's mother, who told me in newly learned and still broken English that he had taken a series of shows in Brazil and was to return in ten months, and she gave me the family's address in New Castle. I wrote him. And ten months later the letter was returned unopened in another envelope from his mother, which also contained an announcement from the *New Castle News* regarding the marriage of Jake Russo to Lara Medeiros in

Ipanema. He had done what I'd begged him to do, out in the rain on Owl Swamp Road; he had found someone and given his passion to her."

Colleen looked visibly shaken by the story. She'd come to Toccoa this day to reflect on some important decisions in her life, but she had no idea this was how the day would unfold. Colleen never could have imagined that her grandmother carried these secrets with her all these years, and it would take some time for the young woman to fully process that and all that the story meant. Seeing her granddaughter absorb the emotions of her past, Lily took Colleen's hands in hers.

"I did visit the Visconde de Pirajá, in 1951, right after I got my art degree at the Sorbonne, right before I met your grandfather when he had just started teaching at UGA and who I loved very much, the way, I have no doubt, Jake Russo loved his wife from Brazil."

Stokes was visibly moved by Lily's story. "Excuse me for a moment," Stokes said. She walked out of the room and a few minutes later returned with the framed formula for Lily's Star. She set it on the table, removed it from the frame, and carefully handed it to Lily.

"How did you lose it?" asked Stokes.

"Lost in the storm" was all Lily could say. Clearly there was more on Lily's mind about this, but the other women could see that it was time to let it be.

After sixty-two years, Lily Davis held the formula again in her hands; a gift from a man she knew for four days, days that forever changed her life. Holding it now in her hands, she could still see his face the day he wrote it, when she awoke that day in the cabin. She closed her eyes for a brief moment, letting the rush of memories sweep over her. And then she came back.

Stokes slipped the handwritten formula into a clear archival folder and returned it to Lily.

It was getting late. But before Lily and Colleen left, Stokes produced another clear Ziploc bag and put it on the table. It contained Lily's old oil paints that had also been in the jar. "Lily," Stokes said, touching the old woman's arm. "I thought you might want these, too."

Grateful, Lily picked them up.

Stokes thought about hugging Lily, felt

the urge to do so, but that simply would not have been professional. Instead, Stokes offered her hand, which Lily took respectfully.

On the way out of the train depot, Colleen, who had been atypically quiet, took her grandmother's arm. "Grandma, can I stay with you tonight?"

Lily knew that Colleen had important obligations with her fiancé back in Atlanta, but she did not ask about that. "Of course, dear. You can stay with me as long as you like."

A ROOM OF HER OWN

As Colleen pulled her big company car up to the front of her grandmother's house, she and Lily could see a figure sitting on the front porch. Mouth beginning to fall open as she stared at him, a disconcerting brew of emotions rising, Colleen looked genuinely surprised. Lily saw the hospital parking placard on the new luxury car in front of her house and knew exactly who the tall young man sitting on her front stoop was.

"Looks like you have company, dear," Lily said.

"I can't believe he came up here."

Turning off the ignition, Colleen jumped out of her car, slammed her door shut, jogged around to help her grandmother out, and then they both walked together up the front steps.

Drew Candler, in his slimly tailored tuxedo, collar open, black tie dangling, stood when he saw them. Then he walked down, meeting them at the top of the walkway.

"Good evening, ma'am," he said, very politely.

"Good evening, Andrew," said Lily in a charged way that belied the simple response to his greeting.

"Hi," he said to Colleen, who just looked at him.

After a moment that seemed to go on a little too long for everyone's comfort, "I think I'll go inside and let you two have some time together," Lily said.

Colleen and Drew continued to look at each other as Lily walked into the house.

Leaving her granddaughter and her fiancé alone on the front porch, Lily made a late supper for them in her kitchen. A macaroni and cheese casserole, with fresh handmade pasta and two kinds of North

Georgia farm cheeses, comfort food with an artisan touch. After about an hour, just as the dinner was about ready to come out of the oven, Lily heard the front door open and she went to it.

Colleen walked in, alone. She looked as though she'd been crying.

Lily saw Drew walk down her front steps and head to his car. "He won't be joining us for dinner?"

"No. He has to get back."

Lily did not ask Colleen the thousands of questions that Honey would have asked her. Lily just stood next to her granddaughter, close to her, and Colleen knew that she was not alone, which was all Colleen needed at that time.

They stood together in the open doorway and watched Drew Candler get into his car and drive off.

After a few moments, the wonderful smell from the kitchen pulled Colleen's attention back into the house and she shut the door. "Boy, it smells good in here," said Colleen, turning and heading toward the kitchen.

Colleen took a seat at the kitchen table, one of her favorite places on the planet, and Lily slid the clear folder containing Lily's Star to her.

"I figure, everyone deserves their own star," Lily said. "I want you to have mine."

Colleen was extremely moved, but before she could speak, Lily stood up. "Come with me."

While the casserole stayed warm in the oven, the two headed out the back door of the kitchen.

They walked into the garage and Lily flipped a switch, and bright halogen track lighting illuminated the room. The garage had long ago been converted into a large studio for Lily. Scores of spectacular glass mosaics, some quite large, in various states of completion, filled the room. A three-foot-high mountain of broken bottle glass sat up against a bricked rear wall. An elaborate collection of oil paints and glues and tools of every kind rested on nicely fabricated worktables. Colleen loved coming in here. In fact, this room, and what it represented, was always present in her life, one way or another.

Lily Davis mosaics were quite sought

after throughout the South and increasingly in other parts of the country. Several major galleries carried her work in Charleston, Wilmington, and Hilton Head. Her work had also been acquired by a few prominent private collectors, mostly in Southern California. In more recent years, there was always more demand than she had ability or interest in meeting. Still, Lily worked or spent time in her studio nearly every day of her life when she was home.

Also throughout the studio were numerous framed photographs of inspiring and especially memorable moments over the last sixty years. There were several pictures of Lily with rural folk artists, mostly African Americans, a few Native Americans, in their studios and posing next to their work in Georgia and Tennessee and various parts of the Deep South. It was clear from the photos that Lily had become dear and close friends with these artisans. These sat next to other images taken on Lily's travels, on safari in the Kalahari, in a café in the Saint-Germain-des-Prés, hiking in Tierra del Fuego, skiing in Telluride, drinking Singha on the beach in Koh

Samui, on a dig at the Ziyaret Tepe site in Turkey. In most of the pictures, Lily was smiling, arm in arm, with her husband, a handsome professor of archaeology who beamed with joy and vitality as he shared life's adventures with Lily Davis. In a few of the photos, they gleefully held a small bright-eyed child, Colleen's mother. Honey's framed photo of Jonathan that once sat on the jade-topped table in the foyer at Holly Hills now rested on a large oak writing desk on the far side of Lily's studio.

Lily walked over to the desk, reached into the drawer, and removed an old sealed envelope. With tears in her eyes, she made her way back to where Colleen was standing and handed her the envelope.

"Somehow, keeping this closed all these years . . . it always made it . . . well, it just felt right to keep it closed. But I think it's time to open it."

Colleen turned the envelope over in her hands, seeing the three-cent stamp, and the address: Jake Russo, 577 Benjamin Franklin Highway, New Castle, Pennsylvania. From the expression on her grandmother's face, Colleen immediately understood why Lily had to keep it closed through her life. Probably for the same reasons, Colleen guessed, that Jake Russo never tried to track Lily down.

Lily picked up a long silver letter opener, carefully inserted the tip in the envelope, and opened it. She removed a piece of fine ivory stationery, which matched the envelope, upon which a note had been handwritten in black ink. Lily set the paper down on a worktable and they stood over it and read it together.

My darling Jake, it has been over a month since your all too short time in Toccoa. So many things have happened since you were here, but my feelings for you remain. Even stronger, if that is possible. How do I begin to fill you in on all that has transpired? My husband, Paul, is gone. His plane went down the day he was to arrive home, trapped by the same storm that blanketed us while we made love throughout our last splendorous night in the cabin. I hope and pray that you will be able to understand the guilt that I felt as well as my responsibilities at that very dark hour which restrained me from coming to you. Since tending to family obligations, my attempts at finding you have led me to your sweet mother, who was so kind as to provide me with your address as well as the news that you have gone to Brazil ahead of schedule. Naturally I am saddened that I cannot share that glorious experience with you, but my spirits are uplifted when I think of you in our flat near Ipanema Beach.

There is something else I feel I must share with you. Upon returning from graveside duties out-of-town, my very first stop back in Toccoa was at our cabin—it will forever be ours!—to retrieve Lily's Star. I am sad to report that the storm caused the creek to overflow its banks and seep into the cabin's foundation. The outer wall of the clay hole where the jar was placed broke open and the jar has disappeared, presumably in the kudzu. I have spent several days searching for it among the vines, but I have yet to find it. But I intend to keep searching.

Lily remembered those days searching for the lost jar that contained the formula.

After everything she had been through, Paul's death and finding and losing love so quickly and passionately, the discovery that Jake's gift was lost put her over the edge. She spent an entire day and some of the night literally tearing through the kudzu with her bare hands, which were soon bleeding. She used her pole to tear up the roots and try to pull the kudzu back. She eventually returned with a shovel and spent two more days doing battle, removing as much of the wild rambling vine as she possibly could. Alone in the forest, exhausted and blistered and bleeding, much of the vine torn up but not all of it, Lily had no choice but to finally resign herself to the loss.

I know if I could hold your most beautiful gift in my hands, it would make the days without you pass more quickly. I count these days, and the hours, and the seconds remaining until you return, and only hope that along with forgiving me for not returning to you, you will disregard my silly girlish entreaties to find another. I do not think I can bear to lose you again. As insufferable as ten months without your touch and your smile and your eyes will be, thinking of what lies ahead for us will make it endurable. As will the memories I have of you, forever in mind, and the moments I hold, forever in my heart. I wait breathlessly for you. I love you utterly and without any constraints.

Yours, Lily

Colleen thought she knew her grand-mother, thought she knew everything about her family. Until this very moment, she had no idea how little she really knew.

Despite the anguish teeming out of the letter, perhaps because of it, Lily was fi-nally left with a renewed sense of peace, something she had made a long time ago with the events of July 1945. For Lily, Jake Russo never aged, never became gray, never changed in any way. In many ways, throughout her life, Jake Russo was an idea. A beautiful idea. One that trans-formed her and stayed with her always. He was like his fireworks. A moment that lasted forever.

Lily folded up the letter, put it in the

envelope, and put it back where it had been for so many years.

At the house, Lily and Colleen refolded the wedding dress and placed it back in the box as best they could, its future yet to be decided. Then it was time to eat.

They sat on the front porch and ate their mac and cheese and drank real Coca-Colas and looked out at the stars over Toccoa.

EPILOGUE

After meeting Lily Davis, Capt. Carol Stokes at the Stephens County Historical Society did some research on her own regarding Jake Russo. Part of this was professional work. Part of it, frankly, was of a personal nature for Captain Stokes. She felt she "needed to know" what happened to Mr. Russo. In early 2008, Captain Stokes passed some information on to Mrs. Davis regarding Jake Russo's life and career. After spending many years traveling the world and shooting shows, much of them with his wife, he settled down with her outside of New Castle and expanded the company business. Over the years Russo Fireworks designed and produced countless pyrotechnics shows, including several for presidential inaugurations. Jake Russo died in the fall of 2004. He was survived by three children and six grandchildren.

A few weeks after passing along that initial information, Captain Stokes received an e-mail from a man who had provided day labor at the Nantucket Island fireworks display in the summer of 1945, an especially large and extravagant show. He remembered Jake Russo, who had hired him to help bury mortars. But what he remembered most, what people on the island talked about for years, was a single firework that was displayed at the very end of the show—a great blue firework, with "the fire of blue sapphires." The man said he asked Jake about it, who simply said that "he wanted to see someone's eyes one more time." Stokes was very pleased to share this new information with Mrs. Davis.

In July 2008, Lily Davis died in her home. The certificate from the State of Georgia attributed the reason for her passing to "natural causes." She was laid to rest in

Toccoa, next to her second husband, not far from the remaining acreage of Holly Hills.

Since that time, Captain Stokes has been unable to find any other record of a blue firework ever displayed in this country that was even remotely like the one shot on Nantucket in the summer of 1945.

In the end, Jake Russo gave his heart to a woman from Brazil whom he met and loved. But he gave his greatest firework to Lily Davis Woodward of Toccoa, Georgia. Lily died knowing this.

Acknowledgments

I've learned a lot while working on this book. Along with the fascinating details of the worlds which I researched and in which I became enmeshed, I've come to understand that the process of writing a novel is by no means a solitary endeavor. Though I wrote much of this book sitting by myself in a small room, I was never alone. On the contrary, from those who shared their stories and opened their hearts to those who made it possible for me to work in that room, so many people are responsible for this book, and so many people have touched my life through the process of creating it.

I especially want to thank my brilliant, generous, inspiring, and tough editor, Katie Gilligan, as well as the amazing team at St. Martin's: Sally Richardson, Pete Wolverton, Matt Baldacci, John Murphy, Dori Weintraub, Joe Rinaldi, Stephen Lee, Lisa Senz, Sarah Goldstein, and the person with the red pencil.

I also especially want to thank my friend and very wise agent, Daniel Greenberg, for nudging me along in this direction, as well as Beth Fisher, Monika Verma, Sasha Raskin, and the entire wonderfully supportive team at Levine Greenberg.

I am deeply appreciative of all the help I received from so many people in Toccoa, Georgia. Marvin and Dolly Tabor. Connie Tabor and Sharon Crosby with the Toccoa Main Street Program. Betty, Patty, Harry, and everyone at Troup's. Thanks to *The Toccoa Record* and the good folks at the Cornerstone Restaurant on Doyle. Jessica Handwork at Ash-ling Booksellers. Shawn Apostel, Brenda Carlan, Sara Merck, Dale Moseley, and everyone at the Stephens County Historical Society and the Currahee Military Museum. Special thanks go to all the veterans who shared their time and tales with me, especially those with the 506th, 501st, 511th, 517th, and 295th companies.

My gratitude also goes to all those in Lawrence County and New Castle, Pennsylvania, who took me into their pyrotechnics factories and their lives. Connie, George "Boom-Boom," Marcy, and the entire Zambelli clan. Vic Laurenza, Stephen J., the entire Vitale family, and everyone at Pyrotecnico. Thanks also to everyone at the American Pyrotechnics Association.

Thanks to my readers Jennifer Dail, Lisa Russel, Ralph Wilson, and Lora Sommer. Italian professor Federica Santini. My pal Michael Koziol. And the experts at the KSU Holocaust museum. Thanks also to my wonderful circles of friends and fellow travelers in the very special communities in Dunwoody, Sandy Springs, East Cobb, Roswell, and Kennesaw, Georgia.

And my deepest gratitude to my family, Joel and Elaine, Peggy Tabor Miller, and Mike and Tara and Scott and Jody and all their associated units. Sophie, Charlotte, Eli, and, finally, thank you to Elizabeth, my wife. Thank you for your ruthless notes. Thank you for those great midnight conversations in our closet. Whether you're in that little black dress or covered in strained peas, you're the most beautiful, wonderful woman in the world. Every day you take my breath away.